AN ENDANGERED HAPPINESS

AN ENDANGERED HAPPINESS

A NOVELLA

and
Seven Stories

PENELOPE BENNETT

HAMISH HAMILTON · LONDON

HAMISH HAMILTON LTD

Published by the Penguin Group
27 Wrights Lane, London W8 5TZ, England
Viking Penguin Inc., 40 West 23rd Street, New York, New York 10010, USA
Penguin Books Australia Ltd, Ringwood, Victoria, Australia
Penguin Books Canada Ltd, 2801 John Street, Markham, Ontario, Canada L3R 1B4
Penguin Books (NZ) Ltd, 182–190 Wairau Road, Auckland 10, New Zealand

Penguin Books Ltd, Registered Offices: Harmondsworth, Middlesex, England

This collection first published in Great Britain by Hamish Hamilton Ltd 1990

Filmset in Monophoto Bembo

Printed in Great Britain by
Richard Clay Ltd, Bungay, Suffolk

A CIP catalogue record of this book is available from the British Library

ISBN 0–241–12959–1

To my Mother with love

Contents

Acknowledgements

The following stories have been previously published, some of them in slightly different forms: 'The Butcher's Christmas Story' in *Harpers and Queen*, 'The Trials' in *Encounter*, 'Mrs F. Pearson-Bent' in *New Mexico Quarterly*, 'The Child Who Couldn't Answer' in the *PEN* (Winner of the Rona Randall Short Story Prize) and 'Out of the Looking Glass' in *Pick of Today's Short Stories*.

AN ENDANGERED HAPPINESS

Part One

Even at night the Hon. Constance Fann's house could be seen. Its tall walls were covered with Virginia creeper which grew right up to its chimney like a thick polo-neck jumper, causing the house to quiver and undulate, in scarlet. Nearby stood a greenhouse. Some of its glinting panes had fallen out, and lush plants now grew through the gaps. Her car was parked on an old Persian rug, within view of her neighbours' bungalow which crouched, sinking or sulking, in a hollow surrounded by a high, meticulously clipped yew hedge.

Between the two houses an oak tree grew, powerfully, both vertically and horizontally, its roots reaching, and perhaps endangering, the foundations of both houses. Despite the admiration lavished on it by Mrs Fann, there was something both alarming and magnificent about the force with which it grew.

In the top room of the house, on a level with the topmost branches of the tree, Constance Fann slept. Her window was wide open, framing the night air. On the mantelpiece was a clock, which struck four – twice – unnoticed by her. In the corner of the room stood a flock of low- and high-heeled shoes, resembling pigeons feeding.

Constance Fann lay sprawled across the four corners of her double bed. She was large and billowy: a galleon berthed for the night. Her auburn hair (which had streaks of grey) frothed out into a copper halo around her head. Her face was white, all her blood being drained into her hectic dreams. A smell of oranges, mixed with darkness, wafted round the room. Before she went to bed, she usually ate oranges, the bitter fruity scent of peel and flesh being released during the night, until it almost awakened her, as it did now. The intriguing combination of orange groves and the Norfolk countryside which surrounded her house made her smile between the sheets – vermilion sheets above which her olive-green eyes peered. Big and bright they were, as though polished with the palm of the hand. And they grew brighter, as from the dense blackness of the tree the dawn chorus began, starting with small excited pipings, small as unfurled spring leaves. Then one invisible bird sang, accompanied by a half-asleep chorus of young damp birds. Mellifluous, concentrated sounds they were, which she would have liked to suck through a straw. On and on the singing went until, later, in the pale navy-blue light, the whole tree bloomed with song.

Absorbed, she basked in the bliss and excitement of the night.

(It was *this* tree, which filled the front windows with its presence – and which she had observed as a child – which had persuaded her, a few months ago, to buy this house and move away from her treeless garden in London.)

Later, from the oak tree's base, came the sound of cat calls, chilling sounds, strong as ammonia, from her neighbours' cat. She heard the sound and shivered.

There were so many things that she enjoyed doing – apart from her sculpture and the selling of samphire – that she could hardly wait to get up. So she leapt out of the bed, leaving it rocking.

Naked, she strode to the bathroom, the floorboards trembling beneath her powerful tread, the dark furniture seeming to retreat at the approach of her opulent white body which resembled that of a (retired) Rubenesque angel – though she was far from ethereal or weightless. She weighed at least twelve stone and had strong bones.

She turned the bath taps on, poured pine bubble-bath liquid into the churning water, and stepped into the scented cloud of foam. Down the overflow pipe, frothy water gurgled. She lay back and smiled, a charming smile which she might have smiled when asleep. She closed her eyes and behind the shade of her lids imagined she was inside a pine forest, where the spaces between the trees were as thick as trees, with the scent of leaking sap.

'Mrs Fann!' A muffled voice, minus a body, shouted in the bathroom. It came from the garden, up through the overflow pipe. It was the voice of her neighbour, Mrs Perkins. Constance Fann surfaced, whale-like, from the water and, covered in foam, leant conversationally towards the overflow hole.

'Good morning to you,' she addressed it vivaciously, wondering if this was how the previous owners of the house had communicated.

'Pardon *me*,' Mrs Perkins's refined voice continued in a well-rehearsed sentence. 'But I think I should bring it to your attention, that a *flood* of your bubbles has reached the *out*skirts of *our* yew hedge. Again!'

'Apologies, apologies. I *am* sorry,' Mrs Fann answered concernedly. There was no reply. 'I fear there's a faulty connection,' she couldn't resist adding. 'But as soon as I've finished bathing, I intend to make Sandel some bread.'

Sandel, Mrs Perkins's only son, was twenty-nine years old and lived and worked at home.

There was still no answer. Just a gust of air from the garden below.

Constance Fann stepped back into the sinking foam. Her neighbours (at least Mrs Perkins) were not, she had already realized, ideal. But if she remembered to restrain the bath bubbles, she saw no reason why they should not get on amicably. And there was always the presence of the oak tree to divide, screen and pacify. After a few minutes she got out of the bath, dried, sprinkled herself liberally with talcum powder and returned to her bedroom, leaving a trail of white footprints.

In black underwear she dressed, the blackness making her feel contained. Then she put on her stockings, enjoying the luxurious feeling of her legs swishing beneath the silky petticoat.

From an ordinary wardrobe she took out her extraordinary clothes. Most of them she had made herself and were variations on the poncho theme, requiring only a slit in the centre of the material for the head to pass through. The edges were tacked together with wide-apart stitches, resembling the footprints of some long-distance runner. The orange poncho dress, which she slipped over her head, had an extra-wide slit (she had been unable to stop snipping, it was so enjoyable) and so was rather *décolleté*, the result being both seductive and, unbeknown to her, intimidating. She then stepped into a pair of red, blue-lined shoes, the insides of which were smooth, and filled with a faint blue light: quite mysterious, she thought, almost feeling the light on her feet. From a giant bottle she poured palmfuls of eau-de-Cologne, distributing it generously. Then she went downstairs, followed by the scent.

She opened wide the door to her garden and looked, with large eyes, at her studio. She was longing to start work – a commissioned male clay torso, which was supposed to be finished in one month's time. After weeks of carrying the idea of it around inside her, and doing hundreds of sketches, it had at last become ripe, and she had at last been ready to begin. But, even then, despite wanting to begin, she had had to force herself into the icy water of that first plunge.

Before she could start work today, it was 'business time'. She went to her garage and filled a high-wheeled pram with underpriced bundles of samphire – a slim shiny succulent vegetable which she enjoyed gathering from the seashore. (It, and her sculpture, supplemented her modest private income.) She pushed the pram maternally down the path, crunching the edible-sounding gravel, and left it facing the road which led to the village. A sign, propped up in the hood, announced: '*Delicious* Samphire For Sale. Please leave contribution in pram.' It was written in large lively handwriting which looked as if it had emerged from something more explosive than a Parker pen.

She then rushed back to her kitchen to make the bread for Sandel Perkins. She should, she knew, have visited her neighbours before now, apart from just greeting them in the village, but she had been too busy. She decided to make specially buoyant bread, because Sandel's spirit seemed pressed down and somewhat yeastless, which, combined with his youth, worried and saddened her.

She dashed outside again and opened the door of a refrigerator (disconnected) in which, for the moment, she kept her cookery books. When she had decided on the recipe, her warm long-fingered hands dived into the flour bin, burying themselves in the coolness and softness, as she scooped out the flour. Every time she made bread, she felt she was being drawn into some ancient, and in a way sacred, rite.

While waiting for the dough to rise, she turned on the gramophone, and a Bach organ concerto began to flood the kitchen, entering her body, until she was filled with music. Then she prepared the birds' breakfast, cutting, in time with the music, the bread crusts which she had soaked to prevent the birds from scratching their throats. She was sorry that the Perkins had no birds to feed. Sandel looked like a potential bird-feeder. Sometimes she distributed crumbs between their yew trees. But the birds never flew there, although the crumbs disappeared instantly.

Surrounded by the fragrance from the baking bread, she made herself some Russian tea in a glass, watching the lemon slice sink slowly to the bottom of the amber pond. While drinking the tea, she prepared an omelette, delighting in the private light which was contained within the egg shells: shells which were almost too fragile to touch and made her want to crush them: absorb them into the palm of her hand.

She was immersed in the beauty and seriousness of the objects she touched.

Before going to the studio, she carried the still-warm loaf through her garden to the Perkins's bungalow.

In the cave-like recess of her north-facing lounge, Joy Perkins and her cat, Dawn, sat watching the television. Its strange aquarium–glow was the only source of light, though this was blinkered by doors on either side of the cabinet. Immersed in her world of a.m. television, she was oblivious of the sunshine which was already knee-deep outside; and of the ringing of her doorbell.

Mrs Fann peered as discreetly as she could through the letter-box flap, into a letter basket. This, too, was dark inside.

But Dawn heard her and jumped down from the chair.

'Sandel! It's probably Lady Bountiful with *your* bread!' Mrs Perkins called out, before getting up.

'Oh, don't speak so loudly, she might hear.'

Mrs Fann didn't hear. But when the front door was sharply opened, the smiles of the two women clashed: Joy Perkins's switched-on and immaculate, Constance Fann's ingenuous, its source mysterious. Despite being thin, Mrs Perkins blocked the doorway, her little fistful of hurt-looking features gathered together in the middle of her face.

Mrs Fann handed her the bread.

'I *do* apologize for the bubbles. But I *do* hope that Sandel will enjoy this,' she said enthusiastically.

'Oh, thanks ever so.'

Joy Perkins was gratified but embarrassed by the apology, her embarrassment annoying her. She held the lopsided loaf away from her chest where, suspended on cords from her collar, two nylon-fur pom-poms boxed at her breastless chest. Constance Fann looked at the hands which held her bread. The small fingers ended in filed-down triangles varnished in ox-blood red.

'Are we keeping well, then?' Mrs Perkins tried to distract Mrs Fann's gaze.

'Splendid. And what a splendid day it is!'

Constance Fann looked round at her part of the garden which overflowed with growth, her gaze coming to rest on the oak tree. Joy Perkins observed the direction of her gaze.

'True,' she commented cautiously, peering at the profusion of unruly plants over the rims of her spectacles. Despite herself, she couldn't help being momentarily touched by something radiant in Mrs Fann which matched the abundant garden. She looked almost starry-eyed. Probably, thought Joy Perkins, quickly and excitedly, she's up to a bit of hanky-panky! For a second she almost considered inviting her in for a cup of tea. For *her* tea-set was certainly up to entertaining Honourables or anyone else for that matter. Specially when she considered the state of Mrs Fann's china cupboard, where not one cup was related to a saucer by birth in the same kiln. It was (as Mrs Fann had admitted herself) like a china orphanage! One, uninvited, visit to her kitchen had shown her that.

Quickly she marshalled her straying thoughts together. It

wasn't only Mrs Fann's disorderly china cupboard which unsettled and irritated her, but also her unnecessary happiness. It wasn't nice or normal to be always happy – for no reason. Well, no reason she could think of. It wasn't lady-like, neither. But then what did Mrs Fann know about that? Even if she was forgetful of her title, Mrs Perkins was not. *She* wouldn't look a gift horse in the mouth, even if it was inherited. It was rude and ungrateful – typical of her class. With nostalgia, she remembered her previous neighbours, the Dugs, who had kept the garden immaculately. But then Douglas was a retired Cemetery and Crematorium Super-intendent, and so knew how to keep things spick and span. And look at the place, after only two months! It was crying out to be pruned – now. Which reminded her that today she was going to do one of her favourite jobs.

So she would not, she concluded, invite Mrs Fann in for a cup of tea or anything else. There was something peculiar about her which she didn't want permeating her premises – or her life with Sandel. He'd had enough of that from his father. (It was Sidney, her *ex*-husband, who had chosen Sandel's name.)

'Well, thanks very much, then,' she said, surprised to see Mrs Fann already billowing away down the path towards her studio, where she turned to wave to Sandel, who, ghost-like, had appeared at the lounge window.

Joy Perkins closed the door firmly. Her anger did not come out in the banging of doors.

Sandel relieved his mother of the bread, smiling to himself in the passage whose dimness discreetly hid his smile. Although he had hardly seen Mrs Fann during the last months, there was something about her which always made him smile – inwardly.

He carried the loaf into the kitchen and placed it on the work-surface, the table having been banished when his mother had redecorated the room. Now, the all-white kitchen consisted of a concealed cooker, concealed sink-unit and concealed refrigerator. In fact everything was concealed except for the stark emptiness of the room – and a caged myna bird called Eileen.

Joy Perkins watched Mrs Fann's buoyantly retreating figure until it was out of sight behind the yew hedge – as though the hedge had swallowed her up – and her garden and bungalow were restored to normality. And silence – the only sound being her sigh, which she didn't hear, against the window pane, as she re-elevated her dyed blonde bouffant hair, at the top of which some reddish strands were visible, resembling rust.

Then she went to the kitchen where, to her surprise, she caught sight of her son's thinness through the many, intentional, holes in his aertex shirt, as he stood against the window. The sight caused a stab of inexplicable guilt.

'Sandel?'

Her voice ventured forth beneficently, attempting a fresh start to their interrupted morning. But then she saw the bread, large and obtrusive in her kitchen.

'Oh, put it where it belongs, in the dustbin, dear. It's that hand-made stuff.'

Sandel didn't move. He could, she remembered, be difficult. He'd revealed the first signs of rebelliousness years ago, under his father's influence.

'It isn't doing anyone any harm.'

'It won't do them any good, neither.'

'Well, it was kind . . .'

'Kind! Fancy giving someone something empty – except for yeast. And carrying it round hot, too – in the open. It'd blow you up like an airship!'

Mrs Perkins, deciding that she would have to put a stop to this bread-delivery business, marched the loaf outside the back door where a row of gleaming dustbins stood to attention. 'There!' she said, lifting a dustbin lid while turning round to see if she was being watched. 'That's that!' She replaced the lid firmly, banishing the irritations of the morning.

She returned to the kitchen, where a fly – the sound of summer in its buzzing wings – flew.

'And you can go, too!' she addressed it, snatched a fly-swat and (resembling an early Wimbledon champion) swatted it.

Sandel Perkins left the kitchen at the same moment.

'Sandel!' Eileen screeched after him, in a voice remarkably similar to his mother's.

Sandel returned to his small room and closed the door, almost – the gap between door and frame being filled by his reluctance, yet desire, to shut out his mother, and by his hope that through the gap some warmth, something, might one day waft.

He sat down at his desk. The chair he sat on had been upholstered in what resembled mole-skin. Most of the bungalow had been furnished and decorated in varying shades of mole, except for one wall of his room which, years ago, in a burst of enthusiasm (he thought it was) he had started to paint red. The result, though, had been more akin to a spurt of blood than anything produced by Dulux. His mother had been horrified and had made him cover it up. But the redness persisted to show through.

Sandel, who was an unchartered accountant, opened a folder of accounts, pending. Instead of figures, he saw the bread in the dustbin. What remained of the smile he had smiled in the passage faded into seriousness. Bewildered, he pushed his hands through his hair; shortish hair which grew in whirls, similar to guinea-pigs' fur. His wide-apart eyes, which each had a different expression, one soft, one guarded, looked out at the garden: at the ornamental bridge which led nowhere and beneath which no water flowed. But it was the tropical forest of the rhubarb patch which drew his gaze. In the early morning, while his mother was still asleep, he had worked there, kneeling among the weighty leaves, which creaked when parted, and the luminous red stems, which squeaked when touched. When he was a small boy he had wanted to be a market-gardener. But his mother had said that no son of hers was going to work with 'dirt'; he would be much better off as an accountant, working, preferably, in the comfort of his own home, instead of in a 'germ-infested' office. Even now, though, he felt the same longing, imagining his giant parental fingers planting and transplanting seedlings, and . . . His dream was shattered by the sound of his mother, in the coal shed, furiously shovelling coal into a bucket. Then came the silence in between, while her gloved hand moved away from the bucket before plunging into the black heap again. His mother was always cold, even in summer.

He lowered his head and faced the columns of accountancy figures. Absent-mindedly his fingers curved round a smooth black basalt stone which his father had found for him when he was a boy. But the stone remained cool – the memory of his father almost too distant to recall.

Before commencing her favourite occupation, which she had now been looking forward to for three years, Joy cleaned the bungalow, moving round the rooms swiftly and relentlessly, humming while she worked. For Joy was a keen hummer, if humming is the word to describe the strange sound which issued from her. When she was spoken

to while humming, she generally refrained from using
words to reply, and just hummed an answer.

On the way to the bathroom she closed Sandel's door.
She couldn't bear stray wind in the house and wondered
why he always kept his door open. What did he think doors
were for? Decoration?

The bathroom smelt of drying jumpers, which hung on a
clothes pulley attached to the ceiling: great woollen birds
suspended in flight. The bathroom wasn't really used as a
bathroom because the Perkinses didn't have many baths.
When they did, they were shallow and tepid, just enough to
take the chill off the enamel. So the bath had a cover on it
which was used as an ironing board – Joy being an artist
with an iron. But her talents weren't restricted to ironing;
she was also a gifted user of the crochet hook. A sample of
the latter talent was the pale green acrylic ballroom gown in
which was dressed a doll, called Selina, whose sole purpose
in life was to camouflage the spare roll of lavatory paper
hidden beneath her skirts. Joy looked sharply at Selina. One
of her plastic dancing pumps was missing. Why couldn't
Sandel be more careful in the bathroom? Couldn't he ap-
preciate her Art-work? But Art, she supposed, was beyond
accountants.

A few minutes later, she noticed Selina's shoe, placed
discreetly beside her. Sandel must have picked it up and, not
wanting to meddle with Selina's toilette, just left it there.
Joy felt herself shrivelling inside. *Why* do I do it? she asked
in a small meek voice. Why am I so nasty to him? And
shutting his door like that, on my own flesh and blood. I
must try and stop it. But, at times, her nastiness seemed to
rise almost independently of her, like a cork in water.

Finding the act of apologizing slightly less painful than
the bearing of remorse, she opened Sandel's door, an inch.

'There's going to be jumbo fish-fingers for dinner!'

Fish-fingers were one of his weaknesses, she thought, the

jumbo ones being brought out of the freezer only for birth-days.

Sandel, who had only recently had breakfast and was surrounded by figures, turned round and, bewildered, looked at his mother's face. It was attempting, not success-fully, to smile its most maternal smile.

'Oh,' was all he could think of to reply.

Joy went to the kitchen to comfort herself with her mid-morning break. 'Ten-ses' she called it. After that, she would start her pet pursuit. She poured boiling water onto her breakfast tea-bag, pummelling it free of any vestiges of brown dye, and carried it and a biscuit to the lounge. Then she turned the volume of the television up and slumped down, a yard away from it, on a plastic-covered chair which let out a loud sigh, causing Dawn to look up in astonishment. The 'ten-ses' was supplemented with a daily diet of news from the *Sun*. 'Impotent Rapist Appeals to Victim', she read hungrily, her fingers becoming smudged. Absent-mindedly she aimed the biscuit at her lips, but it collided with her chin. With a dampened finger she searched for any errant crumbs which she popped into her mouth. She loved biscuits. Something inside her was permanently ravenous for sweetness, though she was unaware that no amount of biscuits, cakes, chocolates or puddings could ever satisfy this particular longing – for comfort, as much as sweetness. As she nibbled and read, a herd of heavy-footed plastic elephants continued their motionless route-march across her mantelpiece.

At eleven o'clock, feeling replenished, she moved her chair back to where it belonged with the other members of the suite. They all had wing-backs, resembling horns, and looked ready to charge into the arena of the small room which was carpeted in whirling designs of yellow, pink and green. Apart from the carpet, and one chair, most of the

furnishings were dark and rather serious, as though attempting to keep the room's inhabitants in order. The alien chair
had been bought by Sidney Perkins. It had over-stuffed
cushions, short shaped legs and a gathered skirt-flounce: a
furniture version of a buxom dancer. She shoved it further
into a corner, hearing her own footsteps, lonely and con-
spiratorial. It was odd, she thought, the way that chair
seemed to shift when she had her back turned. But then
look who'd *bought* it! So it wasn't surprising really, the
effect he had on things, even now, years after she had told
him to leave, when she had imagined that Sandel and she
could at last live an orderly life together. Sandel now earned
enough to support them both, in return for being looked
after by her. She looked threateningly at Sidney's chair.
One day, she thought (as she had done many times before)
she would get rid of it. With a duster she flicked at a glass
case of stuffed birds, half expecting them to retaliate: some
had been savage. But they were preserved for ever from
retaliation or any other expression of life, and just glared
down with their predatory glass eyes at the procession of
mouse-size elephants, and Dawn.

Joy opened a large cupboard, smiling into it at its state of
orderliness. She had a weakness for tidying cupboards; in
fact tidying in general.

She took out her Bonsai tools: saw, scissors, tweezers and
root untangling hook. At *last* it was root-pruning time, her
favourite activity. From its midget container, she prised out
Serissa Foetida, which was twenty-eight years old, Sandel's
junior by just nine months. She had snaps of them both,
taken annually. Her favourite was of Sandel, aged six,
peering waif-like out of his new school uniform. (She had
always bought him a bigger size to economize on a year's
growth; though he, like Serissa, had never grown much.)
Beside him leaned S. Foetida whose trunk had been wired
to twist it into the shape she had desired. Twisted trunks

were her favourite Bonsai style. She smiled fondly at the snapshot of her 'babies', admiring the satisfying results of her corrective measures on the wayward tree. In a way, she thought, she had used the same successful techniques on Sandel and Sidney. Being men, they had, of course, needed curbing.

She held the tree upside down and untangled the fragile roots with her hook. As meticulously as a hair stylist she worked, loving the sharp decisive click of the scissors as they snipped. Her face became flushed with the intense pleasure and satisfaction of the work, so that, with her slight body, she resembled a small girl, busy at her favourite forbidden game.

Sometimes she could hardly stop snipping: once she had nearly pruned a plant's life away. As she worked, a foetid smell rose from the roots of the aptly named plant. She felt almost like a surgeon; though surely surgeons would work in better light. She looked up, and then out at the oak tree whose gigantic shadow had the cheek to creep through the gaps in her yew hedge, *and* enter her lounge.

With the saw she lopped one of the branches, to give a wind-swept effect. She'd been longing to do a bit of lopping and had hardly been able to wait for the tree to grow sufficiently large. Then, using grafting wax, she sealed the leaking wound. Serissa had quite a few well-healed scars. They reminded Joy of little pouting mouths.

A sudden breeze, which came from nowhere, stirred the vast oak. Joy looked up again, and this time saw the Hon. Mrs Fann lying beneath its huge bouquet of branches.

'If I could get my pruners on that tree . . .' she said aloud, her small face, in the dark lounge, confronting the tree's vastness. 'It shouldn't be allowed to grow so unruly. It's indecent! The Dugs wouldn't have allowed it!'

'What did you say?' Sandel's head peered round the door. 'What's that awful smell?' It wasn't the smell he disliked so much, as his mother's collection of crippled trees.

'It's your twin. Serissa!' Joy Perkins said jokingly.

Sandel found it impossible to smile in response, and returned to his room.

'And what's more . . .' Through the double glazing Mrs Perkins addressed Mrs Fann, who was lying blissfully stretched out, 'I'd prune you, too, if I could!'

Constance Fann continued to lie beneath the tree, between whose branches the soft light lay suspended, like a hammock. The palms of her hands were pressed against the base of its trunk, seeking to be imprinted and impregnated by the bark.

As she looked up into the cathedral of branches, she felt the tree's strength flowing into her. It made her feel rooted, secure and peaceful – and also to realize how bereft and barren she had felt in her previous treeless garden in London, where everything was being concreted over, until she felt that soon she would hardly be able to breathe. As she lay beneath it, she wished she could pull the great tree down and embrace the trunk, which was four embraces wide, and all the zig-zag, lightning-like branches. Motionless and deeply silent it was above her. Just one twig swayed, where a bird must have landed and then flown, its presence still felt in the gentle swaying.

I shall plant more trees: a small family of oak saplings, she suddenly decided. All around the garden I shall place these providers of strength and peace. They will help to counteract the orderliness of the garden next door, particularly the yew hedge, whose famished, closely-cropped darkness consumes the light, giving out nothing in return – just solemnity and foreboding.

Perhaps Sandel Perkins would like to help to plant the

saplings. Something in the glimpse she had had of him in the morning made her feel that he might like, and need, to do this.

As she lay on the ground, she continued to revolve her clay torso in her mind. Wherever she went – shopping, cooking, bathing – she thought about it (at times almost feeling that she was being thought about by *it*) as she was carried along by its mysterious exciting momentum.

She was ready to begin, and rose up, as though propelled by the sap in the roots beneath her.

But before going to her studio, she needed to walk through her garden. Over leaves she stepped, thinking how strange it was to touch leaves which once had hung high up in the sky – almost like stepping on pieces of sky. Across the overgrown lawn she went, feeling the succulent grass shoots beneath her feet, whose soles would have liked to absorb the greenness.

She bent down to look closely into the dark-eyed centres of some daisies. Apart from the shape, colour and smell of flowers, it was the quietness which radiated from them which always surprised her. She moved on, stopping beside a bush of upturned goblet-shaped flowers which seemed weighed down with scent. Every time she passed, she lifted a heavy white flower and breathed in, inhaling until she was saturated. Quite often she made several excursions a day to the bush, drugged by its scent, which she would have liked to consume, spoonful by spoonful, as well as smell, imagining the taste of the heavy creamy fragrance. Sometimes, she ate the flowers; their satiny petals creaked when she bit into them, tasting of whiteness and coolness.

She then went into her falling-apart greenhouse. Between the raised beds she moved, her fingers trailing in moss as soft as material, while on either side furry-leaved geraniums arched and almost purred, hardly letting her pass. She buried her hands deep in a jungle of spicy tomato plants, popping a warm fruit into her warm mouth.

Hearing a noise, she raised her head and looked through one of the missing panes. From the other side of the yew hedge the sound came. It was a bird being chased, followed by silence, as, silent as the day, the cat stalked its prey.

Constance Fann continued her garden tour, in the orchard, past pear trees which were heavy with triangles of unripe fruit, pendulous as liquid lead. Each time she bit into ripe fruit she was amazed by its sweetness, and could hardly believe that it hadn't been secretly injected. That so much sweetness was stored in the earth astonished her. She leaned towards an apple tree and, without picking, bit into a mouth-high apple, one acid bite, leaving the apple swaying. She could never wait until the orchard fruit was ripe – until it was shot off the trees by the heat and weight of the sun. There were several apples and pears with missing bite-sized pieces, which, she supposed, smiling to herself, might surprise a passer-by. It was tempting to taste fruit while it was still on the tree; it made her feel vaguely like Eve. She leaned forward to take a second bite, but then something made her look up and turn towards the yew hedge where, in its dark dusty shadow, Dawn sat watching her, wiping, with smooth paws, the last remnants of feathers from her mouth.

Constance Fann looked back at the cat. Some cats she loved.

Then she went into her studio.

Deep into the bin of fox-coloured clay she sank her hands, scooping out fistfuls of the voluptuous delicious material. Onto the skeletal armature she continued to press, slap and sometimes throw palmfuls of clay. Her hands, firm and knowing as they felt out and guided the shape, built up the core of the body, establishing its solidity through the vitality of her touch, while being aware that the clay, too, had to have *its* say.

She had always found it intriguing how, at times, the clay refused to be modelled into a particular shape, rebelling beneath her fingers, however much she coaxed and cajoled. It was both maddening and challenging. Today, though, she didn't need to cajole or coax: she and the clay were working together – she hoped.

She worked intensely, oblivious of the world outside. Sometimes, when her breath was held in concentration, she barely breathed.

Seated at his table, Sandel looked down at the column of accountancy figures he had drawn up. Instead of an addition, he saw that he had sketched a flock of ducks swimming off the edge of the page. He got up and, before his mother called him, went outside to the lean-to and removed the jumbo fish-fingers from the freezer. Before going indoors again, he stood in the sunlight for a moment, feeling the stored-up coldness of the house inside his trouser legs.

*

In her studio, Constance Fann looked up, aware that something was missing. It was the sound of her breathing. It was time to stop, she decided, reluctantly, to look away before returning with refreshed eyes.

She left the studio and walked to her garden shed, from whose small window she glimpsed Sandel Perkins. He looked cold, despite the warm weather, and thin, as though he'd been sliced vertically from something bigger. She picked up a bundle of bamboo poles, for marking the position of plants, and emerged from the shed, smiling at him. Sandel smiled back, his smile moving slowly across his teeth, as though his features were unaccustomed to such muscular activity. She continued to walk towards him, like a ship's figurehead, parting the waves of air with her body as she strode forwards.

'I'm going to plant a forest!' she informed him enthusiastically.

Sandel looked bewildered.

'Well, not exactly a forest; just some companions for the oak tree,' she reassured him, concentrating on his left eye which was the softer of the two. But both contained kindness which hovered cautiously in the background. He smelt faintly of pencil-sharpenings and needed airing, she felt, wishing she could hang him on a washing line to toss and blow in the breeze.

'If you have time, perhaps you could kindly help me decide on their positions?'

Sandel didn't reply at first, but looked down at his hands, which, compared to the rest of him, were oddly flushed and embarrassed-looking.

'Where will you start, then?' he asked, jerkily. 'You'll need something to hammer those poles in with,' he continued, avoiding, Constance Fann noticed, without surprise, the more emotional affirmation which her question required. And she wished, suddenly, that she could carefully sandpaper away (using the finest of sandpapers) the timidity in his limbs.

They walked towards the shed. On the way there, she lit a cigarette. A puff of smoke emerged from her lips – an ethereal sculpture which floated in front of her before vanishing.

The garden shed was silent and dimly lit, reminiscent of a small deserted church. But instead of incense, it smelt of stored-up bonfire smoke, apples secretly glowing in green between newspapers, and folded deck-chairs.

'Someone should concoct a perfume from this smell,' Constance Fann suggested. Sandel looked up in astonishment and nearly laughed.

'I'm going to buy the saplings soon, so we should get the tools ready.' Carefully she unbound a spade and fork from their sacking bandages. The fork's prongs were uneven, the spade's tip curved, both having been slowly chewed away by the earth. Between her finger and thumb she felt their steely iciness. From a hook she took down a chopper. 'We can use this to hammer the poles in.'

They returned to the lawn where she stood for a moment, undecided where to place the poles.

'If we throw them up into the air, imagining we're birds or wind distributing seed, then perhaps the poles will land in their rightful places.' Sandel didn't move. He was, she thought, more like a tenant than the owner of his body. She observed him gently.

Then, using energy which looked as if it had been borrowed from someone else, Sandel heaved the bundle of poles into the air, where they erupted in the sky, before landing all over the lawn.

They raised their heads and laughed.

★

In her lounge, Joy placed Serissa Foetida in a shaded position, to convalesce before being returned to her place of honour on the windowsill. Then she went to the freezer to fetch the fish-fingers, only to discover that Sandel had already taken them out – a gesture which made her feel warm and proud.

While returning to the lounge, she caught sight over the top of her yew hedge of the bamboo poles erupting, and her son and the Honourable standing beneath them. But, sealed inside her double-glazed lounge, she didn't hear the sound of their laughter. *What*, she asked (from her obvious position of horticultural superiority), is that barmy woman up to *now*? They appeared to be playing a game of giant spillikins. But Sandel wouldn't be playing it for long: not when he remembered that fish-fingers were in the offing. It took a mother to know that, she reassured herself.

★

When the marking poles had been placed firmly in the ground, Constance Fann suggested that Sandel might like to look at her newest variety of potato. As he could see that she could hardly wait to show him, and as this was the first Potato Invitation he had ever received, he said yes.

'Even their flowers are intriguing: modest, complicated, undemanding – unlike dahlias for instance – yet with a hint of danger, inherited, no doubt, from their deadly nightshade cousin. But the very strangeness of the flowers warns one of that: nectarless blossoms which are *never* visited by insects. However, what the flowers do *not* reveal is the plant's abundant life below the ground.' She placed her hand flat on the earth. 'How *extraordinary* to have discovered the potato,' she said, as much to the earth as to Sandel, whose eyes widened slightly. What a *strange* woman she is, he thought, at the same time discovering that he rather liked the strangeness. She was quite unlike their previous neighbours, the Dugs. He looked up, for a moment wondering where he was, until he saw that the bungalow was still where he had left it.

'Anyway, that's enough talk. There's far too much talk in the world – it's littered with words, don't you think?'

Not daring to add to them, he just nodded.

Then, to his even greater surprise, instead of using a fork to dig up the potatoes, she used her hands. Into the crumbly earth they disappeared, blindfolded by the black soil as they felt out the hidden underground fruit. While he knelt opposite her, shyly observing the seriousness of her expression (which he felt he should not be observing), a smile entered her features. It was the sort of smile which someone, when attached by headphones to a private source of music, might smile. Only she was attached to nothing – just listening to something joyful and exuberant within herself.

From the dark soil she produced two palmfuls of white-fleshed potatoes which exuded the earth's chill and smell.

'Amazing! Always amazing!' she exclaimed. In one hand she held the largest. It rested in her palm, its solidity embraced by her fingers. 'One day I shall sculpt a potato. It is simple, beautiful in its simplicity, basic, yet complex. It fills the whole of one's hand with reassurance. And to think that all this richness lies secretly hidden in cold black earth. Look!' She proffered it.

Sandel drew back, fractionally, not wanting to hurt her. This potato business was a long way away from his market-gardening dreams; yet somehow, in her hands, objects became different. Nevertheless, he reminded himself, she *was* eccentric; quite alien really. Despite this, he couldn't stop watching her, discreetly.

'And look how delectable the earth is, too!' She stooped towards it. 'One could eat it!'

Sandel stood up, alarmed. She lowered her face to the ground, as though praying, and breathed in the dense intimate aroma of freshly turned soil. 'Why don't you gather some potatoes?' she suggested and challenged, enthusiastically.

Sandel eyed the earth dubiously.

'We . . . my mother only eats chips. She doesn't like dealing with unwashed vegetables.'

'But these – and all the vegetables and fruit – are examples of the earth's abundance – its generosity!'

Not wanting to offend the Earth or the Honourable Constance Fann, Sandel knelt and reluctantly entered the soil with his flushed, embarrassed-looking hands. It was like wading through not only thick but also damp darkness – until he felt something solid.

'Oh here's one,' he said, surprised, attempting to hide his unexpected pleasure.

'And now – if you would like –' she said gently, 'you, must see my new variety, Purple Congo. They are not ready yet, though I planted them on Good Friday, when the devil is *supposed* to be busy elsewhere. They're a dark bluish colour, *all* the way through, and apparently especially delicious. But in *what* way, do you imagine?'

Sandel felt incapable of imagining anything; all he could think of was chips, which wasn't very helpful. But surely, he thought, trying to steady himself, a potato's just a potato, really.

She continued: 'Will they be waxy or floury, nutty or smooth-textured?'

Sandel swallowed.

'One thing is certain, their taste will be kind and comforting. Perhaps they were made in this way because the poor have always had to eat so many of them. Now *radishes!*' she exclaimed with such fervour that Sandel stepped back. 'They're arsonists and can cause a revolution (a delightful revolution) inside the mouth. But to return to the potatoes. Did you know that there are many hundreds of varieties? Not just *whites* as they're so imaginatively called – as if there's only one adjective left in the world!' She stopped and looked at Sandel, the weight of her large eyes resting upon him. 'I do *hope* you don't mind me telling you about vegetables, but they are so infinitely fascinating.' To his surprise, she suddenly appeared vulnerable, almost fragile, at the thought of boring him.

'No, it's very interesting.' Sandel suspected that his words sounded empty, but it was all he could think of to reply, as he wasn't accustomed to having vegetable conversations. But he wanted her to continue – about anything.

'Well, now you must excuse me, for I *must* return to my work,' she told him firmly but kindly. 'But soon I shall go and buy the oak saplings. I'll tell you when I have bought them.' She smiled, the smile seeming to stretch all through her.

Alone on the lawn, Sandel tried to remember the Dugs. Had they smiled? He couldn't remember. And suddenly he found he couldn't remember anything. His life felt as if it had been all gathered together into this time he had spent in Mrs Fann's garden.

Holding the potatoes, he walked back across the lawn whose thick turf made the soles of his feet spring. He felt puzzled and happy, wondering why root vegetables should be the cause of his happiness. On his hands he could still feel the peculiar comfort of the earth.

Mrs Fann, he decided (now that he was on his own and at a safe distance), was like a marvellous cupboard full of strange toys; the sort of cupboard which he might have looked into by accident when he was a child – but didn't.

Before entering his mother's garden, he passed between two cypress trees, from which both scent and warmth emanated, like . . .? He wasn't certain what.

In Mrs Perkins's kitchen, four jumbo fish-fingers basked, half-submerged in hot oil. She turned them over to tan on their backs, the gaily spitting oil matching the unexpected pleasure she felt in preparing tea for her son. It was almost as though during the morning's pruning and tidying, a catharsis had taken place within her, making the day feel different. Suddenly she realized how pleasant it was to be preparing a meal for a man, for that (she remembered with surprise) was what her twenty-nine-year-old son now was – preferable, in a way, to a husband: easier to manoeuvre. Although she did not like Sandel seeing the Honourable, her eccentricity and her age (which was probably twice that of his) made her harmless. So during dinner, she would *not*, she resolved, mention anything about their spillikin game.

In a small silver-plated tray which hung above the sink, she unexpectedly caught sight of herself. She looked back at the tray, to verify that her sudden sense of well-being had been observed by the silver. But it had not. Her face looked troubled; but then the tray probably needed re-plating.

On the naked formica work-top she laid knives, forks and spoons, which, marooned far apart, emitted a dull stainless-steel glow. At the side of each fork she placed a serviette – a single sheet of kitchen-roll paper. Pleased by the orderliness of the scene, she completed it with a flourish by adding a brown-petalled dahlia (made of machine-washable material) in a glass vase.

Sandel entered the kitchen with more buoyancy than usual, obviously having smelt the food, thought his mother with satisfaction.

'Mr Perkins! Mr Perkins!'

Sandel looked round, perturbed, until he realized it was just Eileen, was the sharpness of whose eyes was not diminished by their smallness.

'Oh shut up, you nitwit!' Mrs Perkins rebuked Eileen, not wanting the scene spoilt by a bird.

Sandel placed his two handfuls of potatoes near side-plates made almost invisible by overlapping slices of already-margarined bread.

'We aren't going to need these *and* chips, dear,' his mother said, her back to him, as she removed, with rubber washing-up gloves, the grubby-looking mole-like objects. 'Maybe we can have them later,' she added doubtfully.

So the Honourable was using her son as a gardener, as well as a playmate!

They sat down opposite each other, eighteen inches of formica separating them.

'*These* are good.' Sandel's fork entered the orange, armour-like crust before reaching the babyish softness of the fish centre.

His mother smiled, knowingly, which had the effect of making her chin square.

'I've made us Angel Delight, too,' she informed him, waiting to receive his smile of approval, this having been the main reason for making the pudding. He did smile – he couldn't help it – his small pleated-together smile which she loved.

'I dug those potatoes up. Sort of,' he couldn't stop himself telling her.

'From the *dirt?*'

'From the earth, yes.'

Joy Perkins received the information concerning the potatoes' underground home of origin with distaste, infinitely preferring her frozen plastic bolsters of already chipped potatoes. But she was still determined to say nothing. They hadn't even reached the sweet stage yet.

Before they did – and while Sandel was still raising the last forkful of finger to his mouth – his mother removed, from beneath his ascending arm, his plate and knife, took it to the sink and plunged it into a waiting bowl of soapy water.

After twenty-nine years, Sandel was accustomed to his mother's washing-up habits. His father, though, had been different. Without even looking up, Sidney Perkins had been able to feel his wife's eyes scanning his plate hungrily, as he approached the last forkfuls of food. It was as bad as being looked at by that bird, Eileen, he used to think. When Joy (imagining she was unobserved) had risen soundlessly from the table, with his right hand he had held onto his plate, not daring to use both knife and fork at once, in case she snatched away his plate while he left it unguarded. 'I haven't *finished* yet!' he'd say. 'I thought plates was for eating off of, not just washing-up. You'll wear the things out one day!' But whatever he said made no difference. She just explained that she couldn't bear crockery and cutlery 'hanging about', and anyway, everything had to be washed-up in the end. 'In the end, yes! But not in the middle of the bloody meal!' he had shouted, distraught, his knuckles whitening as he gripped the china. But, for Joy, the mysterious compulsion of getting everything as swiftly as possible from the table to the sink was obviously of greater importance than anything else.

Outside the kitchen window, small round-fisted clouds boxed at the sun; but it remained bright. Inside, although Sandel longed to tell his mother about his newly discovered potato information, he realized that this was not the moment when she would be most receptive to a vegetable lecture. Also, it would probably detract from her enjoyment of their meal, which he could see she had taken special care to prepare. So instead, he asked: 'Where's pudding, then?'

'The sweet's in the fridge, dear. I've decorated it, too,' Mrs Perkins answered, noticing with satisfaction that he hadn't forgotten it.

From the refrigerator Sandel withdrew two aggressively pink portions of whipped Delight, topped with rigid cream and painfully red glacé cherries.

'We haven't had this for ages.'

'It makes a change. And I thought it would be a treat.'

They slid their spoons in simultaneously, refraining from raising their heads and looking at each other.

A few moments later, her spoon buried deeply and safely inside the Angel, Joy found she was unable to stop herself from asking – as though her words had ripened and were about to drop off her tongue of their own volition: 'And what game were you and the Honourable playing this morning, if I may be so bold as to ask?' She smiled as she spoke, coating her words in a flirtatious softness similar to the pudding's texture.

Sandel (a blob of pure dairy cream on the end of his nose) looked up, surprised at the tone rather than the contents of the question. The cream made him look even more guileless than he usually did, and made his mother *wish* that she hadn't spoken. *You're at it again*, Joy Perkins, she cautioned herself. *Careful now.*

Sandel stood up, the eighteen formica-topped inches between them suddenly seeming to have shrunk.

'We weren't playing any game,' he explained, his hands on the back of the chair, in which position he resembled a little boy. Except now, encircling his wrist was a watch strap, beneath which his pulse beat, invisibly but strongly. Suddenly he knew what the warm-scented cypresses had reminded him of: a woman. His virginal mind (especially in the presence of his mother) snapped shut on the image. And the time he had spent in the garden with Mrs Fann abruptly lost its radiance.

The smile which Joy Perkins had been wearing dropped from her face. She could feel it drop – feel the weight of it – and with it all the pleasure of their meal together.

A small silence began to grow between them, solidifying quickly. To break it, she bit into a ginger-nut biscuit which, unusually for her, she didn't feel like. The biscuit broke the silence, for a few seconds. But then quickly it joined together again. She realized that she was involved in more than she had bargained for. Still, she told herself, she couldn't go on eating biscuits just to break the silence and keep things ticking over. Also, she couldn't let her son get the upper hand, specially when he was standing up.

'Well, I don't know what you was doing. You tell me,' she continued, like a professional ferret. 'Anyway, she's twice your age, if not more.'

'What's *that* got to do with it?' Sandel looked even more astonished, hearing his mother's insinuating voice, while feeling he was being pulled into something which was quite alien to him. 'All we were *doing* was pulling up potatoes and marking positions for the new oak trees.'

'New hoak trees!' Mrs Perkins, when roused, was apt to subtract from, or add to, the English language by an H or two.

'Yes,' Sandel confirmed. 'What's wrong with that?'

'Who does she think she is? Robin Hood?' She scraped back her chair and stood up to gain height. 'I'll tell her where she can plant those trees!'

The meal came to an end. The Angel Delight had hardly been touched.

One afternoon, several days later, Constance Fann carefully bandaged her sculpture with damp cloths and left her studio. She loved this period in her work when, at last certain of its inception, she could leave it for a few hours, like leaving a new lover – knowing that she could safely and jubilantly return. It was a kind of daring (vaguely perverse) teasing out and testing of the work's strength and grip on her, and she on it.

It was this afternoon that she had set aside to go and buy the oak saplings. So she went and opened the door of her car, which exhaled the reliable and enticing smell of old leather. But then she closed it and decided to go on her elderly bicycle, which (rather childishly, she knew) she always thought of as a sort of horse, and the shed where she kept it as a stable.

Feeling the bicycle's springy saddle beneath her, and the reins of its handle-bars in her hands, she set off, dressed in a red summer cape which blew against her, like a splash of paint.

Downhill she flew, parting the air, swallowing mouthfuls of its coolness. The sunlight was cut into slices as it passed through the bicycle spokes, and the countryside whizzed past. Over hedges she looked, into gardens, where old apple trees were full of young apples, and the owners of the gardens were asleep in deck-chairs – the lids covering their sleeping eyes, thin and innocent-looking. Between gaps in net curtains she peered, into rooms where tables had already been laid for high-tea.

For her, bicycling was the nearest equivalent to being a low-flying bird. Above, a skein of geese flew, necks stretched out, wind filtering through their feathers. She could hear it! And stopped, wanting to stand directly beneath the flying geese, wishing she could raise her arm high enough to stroke their feathered bodies. Instead, she picked up a feather from the ground and felt its softness against her lips. Had it *really* passed through and been touched by clouds?

On she sailed, free-wheeling along a flat road, the wind behind her, as if she were being pulled by an invisible cord. In the same direction as the young sweet-corn leaves were being blown, she was blown, her back bent forwards like the silvered leaves – until she glanced round and saw their brilliant green undersides, and her eyes were filled with a wash of green. Into her left ear came the sounds from the field of whispering corn, and, into her right, the impenetrable silence of cabbages growing in unison. She steered towards a puddle, stuck out her legs and rode through it, while two Catherine-wheels of water sprayed out. She had arrived at the nursery.

Half an hour later, she reappeared with a bundle of oak saplings beneath her arm. As she secured them to her bicycle, she felt their slim stems between her fingers, and the weight of their bandaged roots in her palms. With a surge of energy, she set off again, hardly able to wait to get back and plant the saplings.

But the return journey, on another road (she always *had* to try a different road), was uphill, down which a summer wind blew, through which she had to wade, as though a hand was holding her back. At the top of the hill was a cornfield and at its far end a house she would have love to have stayed in. It was thigh-deep in corn which rolled in waves, a golden tide, right up to the front door. Some of the corn had already been made into huge cartwheels; she would have liked to roll them over the field – push them over the horizon.

The whole countryside was so delectable and delicious, she wanted to take it into her arms and make love with it.

Later, as the sun started to descend, she started to ride down hill, the early evening air cool on her arms. Then suddenly her cape blew up, blinding her for a second. In a panic which she found half amusing, she whipped it away from her face, just avoiding a ditch. (Once, due to another cape, she had been knocked down by an ambulance.)

At the bottom of the hill it was even cooler. She stopped cycling and dismounted, tempted by a forest which reached right up to the edge of the main road. Into its trees the last of the bright evening light was seeping. She propped her bicycle against a tree and started to follow the light, wanting to see how far it would penetrate before being swallowed by the darkness of the forest. Where the light stopped, she stopped, feeling a strange warmth surrounding her. It was the warmth of the afternoon (which had already passed but which had been stored up secretly in this private place). She stood quite still, enveloped in the gentle air, while listening to the small chatterings of birds preparing to roost.

Deeper into the silence and dusk she wandered. After a short time, the oak, ash and birch trees thinned out and were abruptly replaced by fir trees. This, she decided, must be Forestry Commission land. Line upon symmetrical line of trees were planted close together. For a few minutes she stood on the edge of this mass of marshalled growth, feeling she was being dared to enter, her skin sensing the darkness exuding from the trees. This, she felt, was the sort of place where storms were brewed up, inside the birdless, leafless depths which were filled with fallen cobwebbed branches: and something else less definable. She shivered, unable to continue. So she turned down a path which led to a clearing – and light. Quickly she walked towards it. Then stopped.

It wasn't a clearing. It was a tree mortuary, hidden from the public. Vast ancient trunks lay horizontal, skinned of their bark, naked and pale, their rootless sawn ends bleeding sap, their lopped branches now wilted bushes, the bases of their trunks ripped from the ground, resembling gigantic upturned elephant feet.

Constance Fann stood among the carcases. The loveliness of the day had suddenly vanished.

Gently and firmly she laid her hand on one of the trees, looking as though she was feeling its pulse. Up its whole length she moved until she reached its topmost branches. Here, she told herself, birds had landed, sung, roosted and perhaps nested. East winds had touched these branches, and lightning had flashed through them. She had never touched the topmost branches of a tree before.

Shocked, angered and saddened, she left the forest and bicycled quickly home, the saplings secure in her basket, the thought of *her* oak tree comforting her.

Even though it was nearly dark, she decided to plant the saplings immediately.

That same afternoon, Joy Perkins dressed smartly and set off by bus to the local County Council offices: Tree Section.

Before leaving she wrote a shopping list, noticing with distaste that the top of her biro had other peoples' teeth marks and tension bitten into it – Sandel's she supposed, supposing wrongly. They were her own. 'Cakes, Hair-dresser, Council,' she wrote in her small spikey handwriting which resembled barbed wire.

Outside the cake shop a baby in a pushchair smiled at her. Joy didn't smile back. Her afternoon's mission was too serious for such indulgences. Custard tarts, sprinkled with cinnamon, rusted in rows in the window. Her mouth watering, she gazed into the cake display cabinet, feeling she was being sucked into the twelve-inch-deep trough of sweetness and temptation. The custard tarts were Sandel's favourites, though the last thing she should be buying for him now – after last week's little rumpus. But the tarts (or the image of distant Sandel) melted her resolve. It wasn't *his* fault, really, but that *woman's*. She bought two tarts, and bestowed a smile on the baby, whose mouth was occupied by a bun, so already stretched to its limits. Moody things, babies are, she concluded.

Next she went to the hairdresser. It made her quite nostalgic in a way, for the time she had worked in a hairdresser's. She had loved mixing the tints, peroxides and neutralizers, working away in rubber gloves; it reminded her of cooking. But now her visits were restricted to monthly treats. She always dressed specially for them – at least for Trevor, *her* stylist. But then she had to keep smart and attractive, for Sandel's sake, too.

Trevor dabbed her head with strong perm lotion, twisted her hair tightly round dozens of curlers and left her to set. Trevor wasn't as charming as he generally was; they hadn't had their usual intimate conversation. But then, as he often reminded her, he was a Hair Artiste and so was expected to have moods. Her scalp aching from the powerful chemicals, her eyes filled with fumes, she gazed back absent-mindedly at the mirror, her bald-looking head seeming to have shrunk, her coalite-black hair now long extinct beneath countless dyes. For a second she felt almost sorry for the poor little woman who looked back at her ... until she realized it was herself, and adjusted her features. It was like being spied upon, by herself. Why didn't mirrors reflect what she felt – purposeful and buoyed up at the thought of going to the Council – instead of always distorting things?

Sharply, she pulled herself together, and rehearsed what she was going to say to the Council official. She would demand to have Mrs Fann's oak tree cut down. (That would put an end to her sapling-planting plans.) It had never been pruned, even by the Dugs (bless them), so cast untidy shadows. Its leaves fell whenever they felt like it, *not* according to the season. *And*, it had noisy clanging branches. She could already imagine the sympathy in the official's eyes, and was touched by it. He would probably offer her a chair (upholstered), and after she'd informed him of the tree's effect on her T V – she'd seen branch-like shadows on the screen during *Coronation Street* – he would probably offer her a cup of tea.

Her moving reverie was interrupted by a hairdryer buzzer buzzing close to her ear. She jumped. Fifteen minutes later, by which time she thought that most of her hair must have been burned away by the chemicals, Trevor waltzed across the room and, taking her arm (while raising his perfectly-plucked eyebrows at a colleague), escorted her to a basin. Joy, never at a loss on an occasion like this, curtseyed, imagining she was being escorted back to her seat after a dance.

An hour later, her pink scalp aching, she emerged from the salon. She felt a different woman. Joy Perkins looked a different woman.

She then walked to the Council offices, walking silently along the street, only her terylene coat making a slight sound, of static electricity, generated by determination and self-righteousness.

When she arrived, she pushed a bell at the side of a hatch.

Two-thirds of a misted glass window was raised and the mouth and chin of a man from the Tree Section appeared.

'Good afternoon, I should like to know what to do concerning an outsize tree what is impinging on my land.' She was proud of 'im*ping*ing' and stretched it out.

'Yes, madam. What species is it?'

'Species? Hoak,' she replied, putting him in his place, arboriculturally.

'And what do you want to do to it?'

'Have it cut down. Completely.'

'Well, first you'd have to ascertain if it's subject to a T.P.O.'

'A what?' The conversation wasn't going as she'd anticipated. Where was the comfy chair she'd imagined? Instead, she had to half-crouch, semi-crippled, to speak through this hatch-arrangement to half-a-man.

'It's a Tree Preservation Order.'

'Preservation? It's a tree not a building.' She wondered if she was in the right department.

'And where exactly is the said tree?'

Mrs Perkins looked at him with the steady piercing eyes of the blind.

'In the garden!'

'I'm just stating the facts, madam,' the semi-invisible man said to the brilliantly-lipsticked mouth. 'If it's subject to a T.P.O, or is in adjoining land, it is an offence to destroy or damage it wilfully, or to fell, lop, top or uproot it, unless it's dead, dying or dangerous.'

'I don't know anything about this lop, flop, dying or dead business. All I want is that *gi*normous tree removed.'

'In any case, these things can take weeks, and first of all we would require written notice stating the reasons for its removal.'

'I've got enough of them. For starters, that tree makes my lounge so dark I can hardly see my own son in it, nor he me.'

The Tree Section man didn't seem overtly sympathetic to this drawback.

'I don't know where you live, but the felling of trees in urban areas is considered a loss of amenity to the public-at-large.'

'My neighbour's not the public-at-large. She's one single person. My son and me is more the public. There's two of us.'

'Then there's the question of size. If the said tree's less than three inches in diameter, at chest height, it's not considered a tree.'

'Whose chest?' She couldn't remember what diameter meant, but continued undeterred. 'It's a hoak tree, the size of an elephant, all the way up – never mind about anyone's chest.'

These *officials*! thought Mrs Perkins. However, she changed her mind, when he presented her with a procedural form. She smiled at him, sorry that the misted glass obscured most of her smile.

The man from the arboricultural section closed the hatch, with relief, thinking that the little woman who had been on the other side of it was like a bundle of kindling wood, brittle and sparky, enough to drive anyone to drink – if not worse. Yet he couldn't help feeling sorry for her.

On the way home, she rehearsed another conversation, this time with Mrs Fann.

She'd tell her all about T.P.O.s and (she glanced at the form) Tree Surgery Contractors, some of whom offered Stump Grinding Services. She'd overwhelm her with arboricultural facts, while reinforcing herself. And with luck, in a few weeks' time, that monster would be felled, which would put an end to the Honourable's forestation plans, and everything else – including her bloody cheerfulness.

As she sat on the bus, she could almost hear the Stump Grinders at work, gnawing the trunk down to lawn-level. She could probably have done it herself – well, with Sandel – if it wasn't so indecently large. After all, arboriculture was in her line, really – just an extension of Bonsai. She'd never thought of herself as a Tree Surgeon, as such, though that's what she obviously was. She'd look at the form, write a letter to the Council and post it tonight. Sandel (she mustn't forget to give him the tart) would help her . . . or perhaps he wouldn't . . . Well he would if he knew what was good for him.

She got off the bus. As she was about to cross the road, she saw something lying on the asphalt. It was a dead rat! She felt sick and fearful, until she realized it was just a rag. Joy often imagined rags and old bits of newspaper were dead animals. She shivered in the warm air, her body looking specially small and thin. Each time the rag-rat episode occurred, she knew it was stupid. But she couldn't seem to help it. She pulled herself together, endeavouring to banish the image.

As she walked up the path to her bungalow, she saw the Hon. Mrs Fann with a bundle beneath her arm.

'Evening,' she said, guilty but triumphant, and smiled, her smile looking as if it had been sweetened with saccharin.

'And good evening to you,' Mrs Fann replied, puzzled by her neighbour's expression, while noticing, as she passed her, that she always smelled faintly of a combination of moth balls and fog.

But why did she look so triumphantly unhappy? By the time Constance Fann had turned to enquire, Mrs Perkins was hidden behind her yew hedge.

The two women entered their front doors.

It felt as though it was going to rain.

Sandel lay in his bed trying to force his way into sleep. Above him, fat raindrops started to fall onto the thin bungalow roof. With a violent movement he tugged at the sheet, endeavouring to cover the end of the eiderdown which kept sliding towards him. Its cold paw-like ends knocked into his face. The eiderdown was a pre-war utility model and smelt as though it was always stored in a drawer. He had mentioned it to his mother. She said that if it had survived the war she didn't see why it should be abandoned now. (As a gesture, though, and to tone in with the reptilian green eiderdown, ten years ago in a sale, she had bought the pale green nylon sheets and pillowcases.) At times Sandel could hardly wait for the outbreak of World War Three and the possibility of new bedding. But at least he was allowed to make his own bed now. When his mother had made it he could hardly get into it; everything was pulled so tightly together, it was like sleeping inside a tourniquet.

Sandel lay motionless, daring anything to move. For a few seconds the rain stopped falling. There was a pause. Then water cascaded from the sky, the drops sounding as if they were all joined together in one sheet, as they landed on the roof.

Curled up inside his bed, his ears covered, he heard again the words his mother had spoken when she had returned from the Council, looking brighter and chirpier than she had for a long time – with an artificial phosphorescent brightness. She had asked him to help her write a letter to the Council concerning the felling of Mrs Fann's oak tree, telling him that she needed a male mind to check the facts. Before she had finished speaking, he had said '*No*', and had gone to bed. How *could* she do this? She was his *mother*. He shrank from the thought, while the weight of the invisible rain pressed upon him.

Then, warily and guiltily, he unwrapped the memory of
Constance Fann, in her garden. It was with surprise, almost
shock, that he overheard himself using her Christian name.
Clearly he could see her, lying blissfully beneath the oak
tree; then radiant, almost beautiful, when she had spoken to
him. He could still feel the force that came from her which,
at this moment, made him want to bury himself even
deeper inside his bed. With the weighty bedding on top of
him and the iron-base frame beneath, he felt squeezed –
between Constance Fann's innocent elation and his mother's
destructive determination.

He closed his eyes, wishing his thoughts would drown in
the falling rain water.

In the silence of the room, he heard a faint man-made-
fibre sound, and then felt the pillow and his head sliding
stealthily towards the edge of the bed. He sat up and threw
the hateful pillow to the ground, and boxed at the dinosaur
eiderdown-paw. Then he jumped out of bed and flung the
bedding to the floor, feeling he'd like to throw everything
out of the French window into the soaking night. As he
stood in his pyjamas by his naked bed, in his small room
which was filled with his anger, his body looked even
thinner than it usually did.

Feeling ridiculous, he sat down, exhausted by his anger,
as though he'd been involved in a marital row rather than a
bedding battle.

Later in the night he lay down on the floor, pulling the
eiderdown on top of himself. From where he lay he could
almost see Mrs Fann's house. It was dark, except for two
top windows: a face whose most striking features are the
eyes.

★

Constance Fann lay in her large bed. Because of the rain she would have to wait until tomorrow to plant the saplings.

She always enjoyed sliding into sleep. It reminded her of stepping slowly into a full warm bath, feeling it flowing up on all sides of her. But tonight she couldn't sleep. Certain sleep, perhaps, could approach only in silence; did the sound of the rain distract it? So she lay and listened to all the different sounds of rain, from the fat drops splashing to the finely shredded mist which landed and fell without sound.

And what shall I think about now? she asked herself in the darkness, feeling how luxurious it was to make a decision. With a measure of discipline, relief and satisfaction, she decided not to think about her sculpture, knowing it was now, comparatively, safe on its own. Instead, she would imagine other sleepers lying in their beds, all tucked up differently, stretched out, curled up or jigsaw-fitting as couples. She loved quietly entering their rooms. Sandel Perkins would lie cocoon-like. And his mother? She couldn't imagine Mrs Perkins. All she could see was the strange expression she had observed in the evening. She left the image – unresolved. But quickly it was replaced by the sight of the slaughtered trees in the forest – raw and brutal – causing her features to tighten in the darkness. She could hardly bear to remember the scene, and so returned to her imaginings.

Some people prayed before sleeping: knees on a carpet, elbows on a bed. Some didn't pray. Some prayed lying down, their expressions too private to imagine. She liked to think of all the trusting sleepers in their beds, held in the palm of the night. She wished she could float over them, unwrinkling foreheads, opening clenched fists, smoothing taut eyelids, trailing a blessing. She was never certain if she knew how to pray. *How* did people pray? What did they *do*? When in a church a congregation was told 'Now let us pray,' she always wondered where everyone had wandered off to, while still kneeling there. She perhaps could pray,

she thought, when she was alone in a church and could feel
its weighty emptiness. One could also pray or praise (perhaps
they were the same) in a vegetable patch: in fact anywhere.

She got up and drew back the curtains. She had to see the
oak tree before she could sleep.

Rain was being flung sideways by the wind, slashing and
soaking the trunk, turning it black, making the muscular
branches glisten, their solidity made almost fluid. She looked
into the blackness which emanated powerfully from it,
confronting her in the night.

She closed one curtain and returned to her bed, longing,
almost nostalgically, for the far-off morning to arrive, when
she could work again.

Slowly sleep rose up around her, until only her head was
awake. Then, one by one, her thoughts dimmed and were
submerged, loosened into dreams, and she slept.

*

In her lounge, Mrs Perkins signed her letter to the Council,
with a flourish she was unaccustomed to making. The
sound of her pen on the paper scratched the silence of the
room. With her small pointed tongue she licked the en-
velope. Then she sat for a moment listening to the rain
cleansing everything, until she too felt, almost, cleansed.
Despite Sandel's refusal to help her, she had discovered that
she had been quite able to write the letter herself, minus a
male mind. In the morning, Sandel would regret his be-
haviour – though he'd be the first to benefit from more
light, when the tree was finally felled.

Feeling cleansed and determined, she put on her mackintosh, opened the front door onto the night and, despite
the lateness of the hour, stepped outside in the direction
of the letter-box. At the same moment, Dawn shot into
the house, her tail as straight as her back; and the rain

increased in intensity, making the darkness twice as black.

'Stupid creature!' Joy addressed the cat who was out of sight.

Hard as stones, the rain fell through the trees, bombarding the ground. She glanced up at the oak tree whose branches were filled with blackness as well as leaves, and went inside again, glad that the darkness was on the other side of the door. Rain, she told herself, would probably blow sideways into the letter-box, wetting her letter. She would post it tomorrow as soon as she got up.

She went quickly to bed, wishing she could leap-frog over the night into the morning.

Within minutes she was asleep.

Next morning, later than usual, Constance Fann was still in her bed, from which, generally, she could hardly wait to leap.

All through the night it had rained, and on into the next day; an inexhaustible pouring, monotonous and heavy. With it had descended a strange pressure, a weight on the spirit, a compress on the body, as though the weather was oozing into her.

Usually, she reminded herself, she loved all weathers, except for certain winds, which blew at the endings of her nerves, causing an uneasiness and irritability to spread all through her.

In and out of the crevices of her memory she searched for the source of the heaviness. For she knew that it was not only caused by the weather. Then, without being summoned, Mrs Perkins's disturbing smile rose again. But why should it disturb? And chill? Finding no answer, she let the image sink.

Sometime later, she got out of bed. I *shall* enjoy the day, she instructed herself. I have a choice. I will light a fire and pretend it is autumn!

After bathing and dressing, she went downstairs, turned on the gramophone and started to listen to a Vivaldi flute concerto. Quickly she turned the gramophone off. At times she was unable to listen to music; it poured into every part of her, making her defenceless against a great tide of sadness which seemed to lurk at the bottom of her. She could still remember when, as a baby, her father had held her in his arms and turned on the wireless to introduce her to Bach. She could recall now the unbearable sensation of sadness – and crying and crying. Sometimes she tried to think through to the source of this unaccountable melancholy which overwhelmed her. Was it a dipping into the surface of the world's well of accumulated sadness – or was it something purely personal?

She went to the fireplace and knelt in front of it, sifting the soft ash. Then, close to her ear she heard the distant sound of a pigeon. As silent as the room surrounding her she became. The cooing was coming from the chimney. One of the pigeons was probably perched on the top of it, its soothing watery voice floating down through the sooty darkness.

Delighted, she rose from the fireplace.

A little later in the morning it was still raining, so she put on her cape and dashed from the house towards the studio. Half-way there she stopped, slipped her hands through the slits in the cape to cool them in the warm rain, and then tasted the wetness on her fingers. Delicious, she found it.

From where she stood she caught sight of the main road, whose gutters were overflowing with bubbling water. She walked towards the road, and stood watching for a few minutes, beneath a bus shelter where a queue of people waited. The rain was forcing itself out of the sky, while the people moved as close as they could, to avoid getting wet, yet avoid touching. Watched critically by the queue, she strode out of the shelter, wanting to be in the midst of the pouring water. So passionate was the force and intensity of the rain (heavy as a lover on her), and so exciting and yet amusing to be a part of it in her soaking clothes, that she laughed out loud.

On the way back to the studio, she saw Sandel Perkins, swathed from head to foot in mackintosh. She beckoned to him, to come and enjoy the weather. She would tell him that she had bought the saplings! But he disappeared into the lean-to. In mid-beckon, she lowered her arm, suddenly conscious of its weight. Perhaps he had not seen her. His eyes had been shaded by his lowered lids. For some reason, the heaviness of his lids weighed upon her, too.

Soaked and steaming she went into the studio, knowing that in the afternoon she would plant the saplings.

Each morning it was both exciting and intimidating to unwrap her sculpture before she started work. Although she was always pleased to be commissioned to make a particular piece, at the same time she hated feeling the 'commission' peering over her shoulder into her privacy. She glanced quickly at the torso, put on a smock and immediately started to work, as if too long a perusal might cause her to lose or stray from her original idea – or be seduced by others. With her thumb she pressed the clay, piece by piece, onto the back of the figure.

The back was the part of the body she liked best to sculpt. It was strong, unprotected, without affectation. But one never sees one's own back, except fleetingly; it might just as well belong to a permanently dressed stranger. And yet it lives a life of its own, revealing more, perhaps, than its owner would care to reveal. And because of its vulnerability, there is something moving about it. Backs, she thought, should always be looked at with compassion.

Then she considered Sandel Perkins: in a sense, she felt, his body is all back. If, for a moment, she could change his body to clay, she would release his crouching shoulders, which sought support and protection from his chest; release his shoulders into the air, giving his body and spirit courage to stride through the day.

She continued to work, her concentration heating her in the north-facing studio.

That afternoon, Constance Fann wrapped up her sculpture and stepped into her garden. It was sapling-planting time at last, her reward for her morning's work. Not that she felt in need of a reward. When she was working well, as she felt, and hoped, she was now, it reminded her of being sealed, day and night, to an obsessive love-affair. She was unable to imagine living without it.

Above her the sky was clear, looking incapable of ever having released a drop from its innocent blueness. From the shed she fetched a trowel and the oak saplings and carried them onto the lawn, whose emerald grass was greener than Winsor and Newton's freshly squeezed paint. Pigeons waded in it, turning their luminous necks and listening, over the blades of grass, to the sound of her trowel as she began to dig.

Carefully she unwrapped the saplings from their sacking, feeling they were still shocked from their uprooting, like feverish patients. As she dug down deeper into the first hole, she bent over and looked into it – and then stopped digging, wondering why its emptiness suddenly seemed to be filling with a disquieting melancholy. The mysterious weight she had felt in the morning had lifted. She could feel its absence, almost physically. But *that*, surely, was something different, something outside her.

She looked into the hole again. It was empty of any of

the happiness she usually felt when planting.

She stood up. Something was not quite right. She would leave the planting until later. She re-bandaged the saplings and returned to her house.

As she stood at the front door, hand on the handle, something warm and persistent pushed against her legs. She looked down. It was Dawn.

'Go away.' Dawn continued weaving a figure-of-eight between Constance Fann's feet. '*Please* go away!'

She quickly entered her front door and closed it.

On the other side of the closed door, Dawn continued to sit.

Sandel sat in his room in the afternoon sun, feeling sick at the memory of his retreat into the lean-to.

Not only had he retreated into that narrow lifeless extension, but he had pretended not to see Mrs Fann when she had beckoned to him in her cape. At that moment he had been about to set off to warn her of his mother's tree-felling plans. But half-way there, guilt, and what he thought was loyalty to his mother, had tugged at him, and he turned back, telling himself that he didn't *really* know what she intended to do. The shame of his cowardice stirred inside him.

But why had Mrs Fann been beckoning to him? To help plant the saplings? Or to share the pleasure of being in the rain? That, he imagined, was the sort of thing she would enjoy. He continued to think about her, his thoughts progressing stealthily at first. *Why* was she so kind? he wondered. Her kindness spread into areas unthought of by other people. Never had he encountered this sort of kindness before. Each time he contemplated it, it surprised him. And then there was this seemingly inexhaustible source of enjoyment within her which permeated everything she did. Sometimes he felt himself being almost swamped by her enthusiasm. But it was so tempting. So beautiful. He could feel its beauty inside him, spreading through him.

In one of the neighbouring gardens, someone started to sweep leaves, the broom moving backwards and forwards, soothing his ears. He wished the sweeping would go on for ever.

The more he thought about Constance Fann, the more, he discovered, he enjoyed doing so, his thoughts floating along, light, airy and buoyed up. *This*, surely, was the effect people should have on one another: they shouldn't shrivel each other up. Sandel continued to bask in his feelings. Never had he met anyone like this before, or even imagined that they had been invented, so never before had he felt these feelings. Yet, he had to admit, she *was* strange, her strangeness intriguing and sometimes alarming him. But why did someone like this live alone? Where was Mr (or whatever his title was) Fann? His mother had told him that she had heard that Mrs Fann had been happily married – for a fortnight – and that now, apparently, she and her husband were still friends. His mother had spat out the word 'friends'. Sandel put this small piece of dubious information to the side of his mind. But he realized that the more he contemplated Constance Fann, the more starved he felt, inwardly. He wanted to quaff her loveliness. Then his feelings retreated. No, he didn't, he decided, that would be too overwhelming. He wanted to sip it drop by drop, feeling it nourishing his ravenous spirit.

He remembered again the time they had laughed together on the lawn, their merged laughter enclosing them. He looked down at his arm. He could still feel the touch of her hand as she had accidentally brushed past him. It had really been more of a passing breeze than a touch, but the ghost of it was still there, even though it had happened more than a week ago. He moved his hand towards the spot, just to see if it felt different . . .

But his thoughts were broken into by a cracking whip-like noise which made him jump, as his mother shook the long passage carpet out of the back door, the great dusty waves billowing out from her furiously shaking hands. His palm gripped the uncrushable basalt stone, seeking its geological support.

Mrs Perkins couldn't understand why, since it was nearly tea-time, Sandel had not *yet* apologized for refusing to help her write the letter to the Council. What was he *doing* in his room, with his unspoken apology? she wondered irritably. It had almost spoilt the pleasure of posting the letter.

When all the energy in her narrow, carpet-shaking wrists was exhausted, she returned the carpet to the floor and went indoors. In the hall she remembered how difficult it sometimes was for Sandel to apologize. Inherited from Sidney that was. So, just for this once, and because she couldn't bear the strain of his silent presence in his silent room any longer, she'd make it easier for him. She put her head round his door and summoning her courage – though why she had to she didn't know, as it was *her* door – she called out, 'Coo-ee!'

Dawn shot out of the room, as though she'd been swooped on by a large bird.

'What have you been up to with Dawn?' she asked semi-playfully.

'Nothing. What could I have been *up to*?' Sandel answered, unusually abruptly.

Quick as a flash, as soon as Joy had entered her son's room, she had noted the softness in his expression. Sandel had looked away, as though the glint in his mother's eyes made him uncomfortable, like the glint from broken glass. She had also noticed the lifeless eiderdown sprawled across his bed.

Easing a little more of herself round the door, she suggested tentatively, 'I was thinking of buying a new eiderdown. In the Sales.' Her use of the past tense was hardly applicable, as the thought had just popped into her head.

'Why? Has War been declared?'

'Pardon?' Magnanimously she ignored his remark. Anyway, she wasn't going to retreat now, with one foot and half a leg in the room. Sandel eyed her legs which were enclosed in puce-coloured stockings, giving the impression that they were blushing, independently of her, at some embarrassment which was taking place higher up in her body. 'Don't you agree – about purchasing an eiderdown?' she prompted. It was unusual for her to seek agreement with anyone but herself. She wished Sandel would stop looking at her legs. It wasn't nice.

Sandel sat far back in a corner of the room, his head bent and in shadow. The silence in the air began to thicken: to coagulate. Joy felt the stirrings of anxiety, and was glad of the support of her (plywood) door. He didn't look like her Sandel today – not like the little boy she had always known. Perhaps he was feeling poorly, she thought in panic. She considered herself automatically as the mainstay of the home. This was probably due to Sandel working so quietly in his room, except when he went out to see his clients. Had he made more noise with his accounts, or gone out to work regularly like anyone normal, it would have been different.

Then she remembered that it was Sandel, after all, who provided their income.

'Why don't you give yourself a break, dear?' she was surprised to hear herself suggesting.

'What sort of break? Another fish-finger banquet?'

'If you like . . .'

'I don't know why you seem to think that fish-fingers mend everything, like some universal glue – even if they taste like it.' Sandel spoke with unaccustomary force.

Surprisingly Joy Perkins's patience persisted, for a few more seconds, she being more offended by his culinary confession than anything else.

'If you don't like *my* catering, dig up some of those old potatoes. Or do some planting with the Honourable,' she suggested blithely.

A silence, dense as a third person, settled between them.

'Well, I was only *suggesting* out of *kindness*,' she added, as a palliative, to dilute her previous sentence, and break the silence.

'*Kindness!*' Sandel gripped the stone, until it looked soldered to his palm. 'What's *kind* about cutting down that tree? Cutting down that woman? Can't you *see* what it means to her? It isn't doing you any harm. You couldn't be harmed!' He looked directly at her. 'That tree,' he informed his mother slowly, 'just gives her happiness.'

'*Happiness!*' Mrs Perkins chortled, the edge of her simulated laughter touched by hysteria. 'What does she know about bloody happiness? What's she got to be happy about, any roads? She's on 'er own, and no wonder. She deserves to be. She's *not* happy! She's barmy. She's not an artiste, neither. She can't even make bread let alone Art. Anyway, what's she doing cooped up in that old shed all day, with bits and pieces of mud bodies lying all over the place? It's like a human abattoir. It's not healthy.' There was a pause which, while she accumulated more breath, she felt obliged to fill. 'And she's irresponsible, too, letting a tree grow so indecent. People like that shouldn't be let loose on the Public. At Large.' Joy Perkins was gaining momentum. 'I hate her bloody happiness!' she shouted. 'She's old enough to be your aunty. Your *great* aunty.' She paused, but not for long. 'And anyway, if she's so *happy*, it's probably because she's having it off with someone – people of her class do, all the time – have a bit on the side.'

'On the side of *what*?'

'Oh, we are posh all of a sudden! Inherited from next door, no doubt.'

'Well, not from you, obviously!' Sandel drew breath. 'She's happy because of her *work*,' he said adamantly, distancing himself from his mother, 'and because . . .' he spoke as though surprised by his own words, 'and because of her garden, not because of *someone*.'

'Oh yes! I wasn't born yesterday!'

'I know.' Sandel looked at her worn, exhausted face.

'*You* know?' she retorted scathingly. 'What would *you* know about such things?' Her words drilled relentlessly into her son, as if they were speaking themselves. 'Well, she's not having it off with one of her old potatoes – I can tell you that! I've seen the way she looks: all gooey-eyed – at *her* age! It's disgusting!'

Suddenly she began to hear her own words. The spaces between them were becoming wider. She was repeating herself, losing momentum. She looked at her son with what could, without difficulty, have been interpreted as hatred. *If I wanted to, I could staple him down with my words: crush him. But he isn't worth having a row with. He just becomes silent. He's a coward: one part man, three parts water. Sidney's son.* She looked at him again. The red pullover he wore clashed with a redness in him which smouldered slowly in the early evening, as he sat bent and dark, the light sparking from his eyes when he moved his head. She looked once more at him. And then retreated from the room, her puce stockings burning, her legs feeling suddenly unsteady.

As she walked determinedly down the passage, she tripped on the carpet.

'Bloody carpet! It's obscene!' She kicked its pile-less surface, painfully jarring her knee.

That night Sandel walked out into the darkness, walking with determination beneath a big bruised moon towards Mrs Fann's letter-box. He was astonished that his anger should provide him with so much courage. In his breast pocket he carried a letter, telling her of his mother's intentions, and saying that he would do what he could to prevent the felling.

For a second he stood facing her house, before quietly pushing open the letter-box flap. As he did so, the tips of his fingers felt the air on the other side of the door. It was warm and tempting, and he longed to put his hands, arms, the whole of himself through the flap and into that mysterious warmth. He wanted to enter and become a part of her rich and private world.

Then he heard the sound of the letter landing on the floor. He withdrew his hand and started to walk back to the bungalow.

He stopped. What would she do when she read the letter? To his amazement, he realized that he hadn't really considered this. He looked back at her house: the windows were without light. Feeling juvenile and hesitant, he continued walking silently towards the bungalow.

And what would his mother do when she heard about the letter? There didn't seem to be sufficient space inside his head to worry about that, too, until the hateful, insinuating words she had spoken about Mrs Fann began to surface from his memory. They weren't true, he told himself, and he didn't care. Despite the lack of space and caring, he couldn't stop himself feeling guilty. Guilt was always there, in one way or another, making itself felt: an inoperable complaint.

Dragging his shadow through the moonlight, he squeezed

his way between the yew hedge, and disappeared into his mother's bungalow.

Alone in her narrow bedroom, Joy sat down on the edge of her single bed. She could still hear the click of the door as Sandel went out into the night. (Probably just for a breather, she explained to herself.) But the clicking door was the loudest sound in the bungalow – that, and the movement of her hand rubbing her still painful knee. Her other hand stroked Dawn's back, with swift, absent-minded strokes.

'Why do I go on doing it?' she grudgingly asked herself. Dawn didn't respond, her concentration focused on being stroked. 'I don't mean to – really – because I love Sandel, don't I? We both do. He'll always be my baby . . .'

Sometimes she felt there was an almost rat-like presence inside her, gnawing away, ever ravenous for a tit-bit of nastiness to chomp and chew on. Against her stomach (which suddenly felt painful) she placed her arm, as if that was where the gnawing took place. With her forefinger she rubbed away at Dawn's forehead, looking as though she was trying to erase a stain, her movements clumsy, the caresses of someone who has never been caressed – even by a cat.

A few minutes later, unable to bear the absent-minded hand any longer, and to remind its owner of what she was supposed to be doing, Dawn nipped Joy Perkins lightly on the wrist. At the same moment the front door clicked and Sandel entered the bungalow, and went to his room.

'You two-faced feral. You're no comfort.' Joy emptied Dawn out of her lap and moved her hand from her stomach to her wrist.

'If only I had something to *chew*,' she said wistfully, a few minutes later, to her bedroom curtains.

AN ENDANGERED HAPPINESS

Part Two

Constance Fann lay in her bedroom.

She wasn't certain how much time had passed – days or perhaps weeks. From the small clock beside her bed, the seconds continued to drip. The room was becoming filled with hours, half hours and minutes which, when she got out of bed, would reach up to her ankles. She lay buried beneath the darkness of her quilt which protected her from the summer day. Sandel Perkins's often-read letter lay beside her.

Through the quilt's duck-feathers sifted the sound of rustling leaves. She raised her heavy eyelids, beneath which she had been trying to sleep and seek shelter – eyelids which looked weighed down. Carefully she lowered a corner of the quilt, and with one large eye looked out at the oak tree, looking deep into its branches into which the pigeons had flown to shelter from the midday sun, their flapping wings parting the heavy summer leaves. For them it was a forest in which they sat slowly rocking and cooing, their grey feathered wings larger than the leaves. She lowered another inch of cover. With her eyes she felt along and around the leaves, imagining how they and the light between them would feel to her touch.

Then she felt the letter, and looked quickly away. Light as a feather it rested on her bed, its contents heavy. She knew from its brevity how much Sandel had hated writing it. Poor boy, she thought tiredly, almost wondering who he was.

Everything felt so distant, it was painful, almost physically painful, to drag from her memory that moment when she had stooped in her passage to pick up his letter . . .

When, on that day, she had finished reading it, she felt that, without warning, she had been attacked.

Knowing only too well how explosive she could be, she had considered it wiser not to go and see Mrs Perkins. Sandel she would thank when she met him in the garden. So reluctantly she had gone to her sitting-room instead of her studio, and with a sense of foreboding which made the receiver feel leaden, she had immediately telephoned her solicitor. (She always dreaded anything to do with litigation.) The law courts, she had been informed by a clerk, had just risen, and Mr Waite, her solicitor, had departed for his holiday, so the office was officially closed. She had explained the problems to him, adding that it was because of the tree that she had bought the house. Silence (compounded of incomprehension and derision) had filled her ear.

'Are you still there?' she had enquired.

'Yes,' replied the clerk, economically.

She had asked if, unofficially, he could kindly look up the file containing the details concerning her house. The semi-somnolent clerk (who also sounded in need of a holiday) had reluctantly agreed. After what had seemed like an hour – while the telephone receiver had been filled with the sound of rustling papers (as though he was wrapping up his Christmas presents) – the clerk had returned. He informed her that he could not locate her file, but recalled that Mr Waite *had* cautioned her concerning the aforementioned tree. (Why can't he speak normally, she had wondered, instead of using this ridiculous dusty language?) And, he had continued, as the tree is, if I'm not mistaken, situated exactly between the two adjoining gardens, if, at any time, either party wanted it felled, the matter would, in all probability, have to be taken to court.

'Well, that is the first time I have ever heard of an oak tree being taken to court.'

The clerk, obviously accustomed to clients' irrelevant responses, had continued as though she had not spoken. At the time, he reminded her, Mr Waite had suggested that it would be prudent to research the matter more thoroughly, *before* the contract was signed. She remembered, quite plainly, how impatient she had been to sign the contract, to move into the house (before anyone else did, as it was the first time, since she had been a child, that it had been put up for sale), and to start work on her already delayed commission. But Mr Waite, she had felt, was not the man with whom one could discuss torsos. So she had instructed him not to undertake any research and to proceed immediately with the signing of the contract.

For her, the mere idea that anyone could contemplate the felling of an oak tree was inconceivable. Trees, she always assumed (especially of this size, age and dignity), belonged to everyone, not to anyone. Like mountains, people and rivers, they were part of the planet. She had managed to refrain from telling this to the clerk, not wanting him to fall completely asleep.

'But what can I do *now*?' she had been unable to stop herself from imploring.

Another long silence had ensued, during which time she began to wonder if he was taking his coffee break.

'On the rare occasions when Mr Waite's instructions have been ignored, and matters of this nature have arisen, we have advised our clients to approach their Local Council, to ascertain if the tree in question is safeguarded by a Protection Order.'

The words 'Protection Order' had made her shiver. What else, apart from the elderly, the landscape, the foetus and animals, would need protecting next? People's smiles?

She had thanked him and replaced the receiver as quickly as she could, glancing at her watch (she had already wasted most of the morning) before lifting the receiver again and dialling the Council.

A bass-voiced answering machine had informed her that the arboricultural staff were not available at the moment, but if she left a message and her name and address they would 'get back to her'.

The answering machine then performed a single-note electronic rendering of a snippet of Vivaldi, simplified to the point of imbecility.

Maddened, she had walked to the window and stared out at the tree. It had been a part of her childhood, her memory of it as vivid as its physical presence. Both, she had always assumed, were invincible.

She had then gone to her studio, and with the threatening weight of the oak's fate hovering over her, had tried to work, while waiting for the Council to telephone.

They did not telephone.

She had considered it pointless to go to the Council herself, if the office was staffed solely by a machine. It was equally pointless to consult another solicitor, unless she had access to the file on her house.

So for several days she had continued to telephone and leave messages, while her anxiety grew in size and weight and her ability to concentrate and work began to crumble.

As the days of being able to do nothing had gathered behind her, she began to dread the disembodied machine-voice and the information it imparted, which bored into her ear.

On one occasion, her voice had thundered back:

'Aren't there any human beings left in the world to answer telephones? Is there a sudden shortage of people?'

. . . are not available at the moment . . .

'At *which* moment are you available, may I ask? It is *not* Sunday, *nor* the middle of the night – as far as I am aware!'

. . . please leave a message . . .

'It is not a *message* I want to leave, confound it! Has the world gone insane?' she had shouted, and had flung the telephone onto the sofa.

After that, she telephoned no more. She began to feel as though an explosion had taken place, causing an implosion within her.

Her shame, at her failure to achieve anything concrete, blackened each day.

The time when the commission had to be completed moved a step nearer each hour. Her work became laboured and painful, until finally it came to a halt.

In the garden the immense tree stood, contained within its own vast stillness.

The silence from the four walls of her room began to surge towards her. *I must get up. I must work.* But neither her body nor her spirit responded. She was empty of energy and happiness. Painfully, she tried to force herself to be tempted by her sculpture. But it was without seduction or echo. Without reason. What was the point of cluttering the world up with one more torso – scooping yet more clay out of the body of the earth? Her desire to continue working had vanished, as though the growing vertical strength in her clay figure had been linked in some way with the tree's vertical strength. *But I must finish.* It's a commission, she warned herself. The word 'commission' produced an instant icy fear from which her thoughts fled, unable to cope.

Instead she looked at her room. Although nothing moved in it, there was, she thought, a wind outside and bits of it (remnants left over from a storm perhaps) were lurking inside her house, so at any moment the wide-open bedroom door might slam: slam on her body which felt fragile, almost feverish and unequipped for such an onslaught.

Before the door banged, she forced herself from her bed and passed, stooping, beneath the door frame on her way to the bathroom. When the bath-water was almost overflowing, she reminded herself to climb into it. She lay there, the water surrounding her depressed limbs, reaching above her closed mouth. *It's high tide*, she informed herself. She didn't seem to hear. *But I must hear.*

Dripping and tired, she rose from the bath; and, partially dried, returned to her bedroom, her body passing through the bodies of warm air around her.

She dressed in black – black clothes to combat the brightness of the day. Then she descended the staircase, holding onto the banisters, as an unsure guest might, in someone else's house. In the kitchen she buttered some bread. As she ate, standing up, the smell of the bread began to invade the room. She was being squeezed out. *I shall go into my garden. But if I leave the house, something, anything, might catch fire. The old Sunday newspapers in the sitting-room might ignite by a mysterious friction – the inflammable crime reports and the obituaries rubbing slowly together.*

Despite the risk, she took an umbrella which had a hole in it and walked into the garden, walking beneath the black, maroon and purple light which filtered through the umbrella panels. She stopped. Something was missing: a part of herself, as if she was only partially dressed. She turned round and looked at her house. But the house was blank. Quite often she had had this sensation of missing something, when leaving buildings. And it was always more than just the absence of a glove or umbrella. But *what* it was she didn't know. Everything was fathoms away, down in her memory, which was now closed, apparently, for the purpose of recall.

Above her, a plane was ploughing up the sky – a great aerial tractor. She was glad of the umbrella. In front of her, a red speckled broom bush shook, without the assistance of a breeze. She quickened her pace, and tripped over a shadow.

Her hands felt tight and her shoes sank in the grass as she walked beneath a beech tree, treading on last year's leaves and nuts. Three leaves blew towards her. Quickly she turned away, holding onto a breeze with her hands as she went round a corner and into her greenhouse. But then quickly she came out again, her forehead bumping into the thick scent of tomatoes. They were suffocating her. Soon the melons would explode with sweetness; she would be bombarded with their seeds.

Trying not to breathe or look, she went into her studio. Briefly, she glanced at the covered torso. She frowned at it. *It has nothing to do with me. It is something which has endeavoured to adopt me. To force itself onto me. I shall destroy it.* She moved towards it. But something was watching her. She looked up and into the face of a sunflower which peered through the window.

In panic, she left the studio.

On the edge of the garden, someone hovered. *That must be the young man who lives next door.* She looked at him vaguely. *What is his name?* She didn't seem to have any names inside her to remember.

She walked across the lawn, between the leaning bamboo poles, which she could hardly bear to look at. Then she stopped at the first of the holes she had started to dig for the saplings. She bent over and looked into it. As she did so, she remembered a name: *Mrs Perkins.*

Very slowly the hole began to fill with the memory of her smile. It was the lethal cheerfulness of it which disturbed and destroyed. With her foot she kicked the soil back into the hole, covering the smile.

She walked away and returned to her house and her bed.

If only, she wished faintly, before burying herself in the safety of sleep, *I could lift for one second the heavy edge of the day and see beneath it.*

Sandel stood, slim and bewildered, on the edge of Mrs Fann's lawn.

After delivering his letter, he had waited for what seemed an immovable mountain of time to pass, either to see or hear from her. But he had heard nothing. She had never appeared. Twice, often three times, a day, he had gone to look at her house, willing an answer from the bricks and mortar. But the house had exuded only silence. What, he wondered constantly and obsessively, had his letter done to her? And was it due to his letter? But there had been nothing with which to grip or tackle the silence. And what was she doing alone inside her silent house? If only he could put his hand through the flap and take back the letter . . . and perhaps feel again that comforting tempting warmth. He had put his hand up to his face, as though steadying himself, and was shocked to feel how young it felt.

Then one day, when walking slowly back across her lawn, he had looked down and suddenly known what he was going to do. He would heel-in the saplings, even though they did not belong to him. He found that he could no longer bear to think of them gasping in the shed.

As he had crouched, trowel in the earth, on her lawn, he had felt once more, with anguish this time, the loveliness of her. If only she would say 'we' to him again, and he could be included *inside* that warm and suddenly most desirable of pronouns. He had longed, with a painful urgency, to see her smile again, to submerge himself in it. Never before, he discovered, had he longed for someone's smile. He remembered watching her face for the first signs of it to break through her seriousness. He could still feel it inside himself – igniting him.

After a time he had stopped digging and raised his head,

feeling he was being observed. He had looked round and seen Dawn watching him, from beneath the yew hedge. Only her eyes had been visible, the darkness of her fur and the density of the yew shadows having swallowed the rest of her.

Just a few yards from this spot, he remembered, he had knelt opposite Mrs Fann and searched for the potatoes. Had that whole episode been wiped out by his letter? Was it now just his solitary memory? It was at that moment that he had sensed something powerful which radiated from her which had tempted and enticed (yet frightened) him, causing a heat as hot as the day to flow through him. Sweat had dripped into the hole, surprising him and making him look up, almost as though it had come from someone else. But it was *his* sweat.

And as he had looked up, there she had been, standing outside her studio.

Dressed all in black in the brilliant sunshine. Why? Had someone died? The shock of the blackness and sombreness of her clothes had caused his momentary happiness slowly to deflate, his rocking heart to grow still. And why had she been holding an open umbrella? He had glanced up to make certain no drops were falling from the hot blue sky. Then, gathering his courage, he had stood up and looked straight at her, his gaze feeling soft, as though his eyes were suddenly lined with velvet. But she had not recognized him. He had touched his forehead, making certain it was there, and stepped towards her. But she had walked slowly away, stopping briefly beneath the oak tree, her expansive body appearing diminished and absorbed by the vastness of the tree.

He had rushed towards his mother's house.

Joy was in her kitchen – at least one of her legs was, the rest of her having disappeared inside a large cupboard in which she was hunting for . . . She couldn't remember what. All she could remember was Sandel. She couldn't stop thinking about him. Although their row had taken place some time ago, she knew that none of the things she had said could be retrieved or erased. It was like posting an angry letter; you could never squeeze your hand into the letter-box to get back the letter. It was *she* who had ended up exhausted and bruised – though triumphant. And, after all, she, like most normal people, needed a proper row-partner. Not someone cushion-ish but someone strong, like herself; not too strong, mind you.

The trouble with the last row was that 'things' hadn't been quite the same since. Sandel was definitely different. She couldn't help being anxious about him. Something was brewing in him which disturbed her, because she had never seen it before. He looked so dark, too: dark with worry. He'd never been a dark-looking boy, and Sidney wasn't dark, you could say that for him.

With a clatter, the rest of Joy disappeared into the cupboard as, with panic, an unexpected thought shot into her mind: Sandel might leave her for ever.

Finding the thought too painful and improbable to consider, she struggled to get herself upright. 'I must get out of here before Sandel appears – or what's left of him to appear.' She looked round. 'Don't just sit there. Help,' she addressed Dawn.

'Help!' repeated Eileen.

'I wasn't speaking to you.' Joy hadn't been speaking to Dawn, either. Since what she called the *attack*, on her wrist, Dawn had been out of favour. But as there was seldom anyone else to speak to, she sometimes forgot, and continued to consult Dawn, who sat, neat and contained, watching her owner, her tail curled over her front paws, resembling a travelling rug.

Joy then saw what she had been looking for. It was the pie-funnel. With a rush of maternal love, generated by the fear of Sandel's departure, she decided to make him a steak-and-kidney pie, accompanied by frozen spinach. And *this* time, she reminded herself, she would not mention a word about his fish-finger confession even though it still stung her. What's more, she'd wash the front doorstep as well.

She almost ran to the freezer, certain that everything would be better from now on.

After preparing the pie, Joy Perkins cleaned her doorstep. While she was squeezing the last drops from her mop, Sandel appeared, running across the lawn. She smiled, her smile suspended above the bucket of twinkling soapy water. Sandel noticed her expression and stopped running.

'I don't think Mrs Fann is well,' he said, out of breath. 'She's dressed all in black . . . and ladies, women, don't wear black, in summer. Do they?'

His mother was still listening to him, he noticed. Why wasn't she *always* like this? 'I don't think she knew who I was,' he continued.

'Let's go in, Sandel, and talk about it.' They moved towards the front door. 'Oh, don't step on the doorstep, dear,' she couldn't help reminding him, at the same time flicking away an ivy tendril which appeared intent on entering her bungalow.

'And I think,' said Sandel, taking one huge stride over the step into the hall, where he was protected by the meagre light from the forty-watt bulb, 'I think it's because of the threat of the tree-felling. I told her about it,' he admitted, his back to her.

They went into the lounge. Sandel stood, feeling awkward, resembling a piece of furniture delivered to the wrong address.

'Sit down, dear,' Joy Perkins invited, her voice, inside her, sounding velvety.

Sandel sat in a corner, on Sidney's chair. *I'm entertaining my son!* Joy realized, with a sudden swelling of pride and pleasure which almost embarrassed her. Sandel shifted forwards, occupying the minimum of upholstery.

'I don't think you should get that tree cut down.'

His sentence landed naked, and without introduction, in the room.

'Why not, Sandel?' Mrs Perkins endeavoured to maintain the velvet tone.

They spoke quietly and warily in the wall-to-wall carpeted lounge.

But it didn't take long for her to realize her position of power, and how delectable this teaspoonful of it tasted. Not that power hadn't been a substantial part of her diet for some time now – since quarter-way through her marriage, really. But this tasted different; and she should know, for she was quite a gourmet in these matters.

'Because it's changed . . .' Sandel was reluctant to use the word waiting on the tip of his tongue; but he could think of no alternative. 'Because it's made her a bit odd. Perhaps.'

'*Made?*'

Sandel was immediately alerted by his mother's unaccustomed meticulousness about the use and tense of words, and retorted sharply and condescendingly, hating and hurting himself:

'Yes. *Made*. I hadn't noticed you were a grammarian.'

Neither had his mother. For all she knew they were some branch of the Rotarians. That was the reward you got for over-educating your offspring. Not without considerable difficulty, she remained silent, employing a patience she was unused to, and had acquired, it seemed, only minutes ago.

There was a pause, during which time Sandel wondered what his mother was thinking.

But Joy, who was never particularly prone to thinking as an activity in itself – especially before speaking – believed that silences were made to be filled, not wasted. So, unable to resist, she addressed herself quietly; just sufficiently quietly to be overheard.

'But she always was odd – a bit. Wasn't she?'

She consulted a black nylon–fur–covered cushion, mistaking it for Dawn.

'She's *not* odd. She might be a bit unusual. In fact she's probably the only really sane person here.'

The more Sandel spoke, the more he realized how like weapons words could be. 'She's just extra sensitive, and this tree-felling threat has probably upset her.' He began to see that his words were true. 'You can't . . .' To his surprise he suddenly found that he could raise his head, look at his mother and speak. 'You can't continue it. *Please* stop before any more damage is done,' he pleaded. 'I don't want to have anything to do with it.'

'Well,' said Joy slowly, savouring the word in her mouth as she would an acid drop. 'I may. And I may not. It all depends.' She smiled a small smile, minute in comparison to the satisfaction she felt, while being oblivious of how dangerous her equivocal reply was.

Sandel felt partially relieved, amazed that no real row had taken place – yet.

Joy discovered, with a sense of relief which astonished her, that, during the past few minutes, she had almost lost interest in the fate of 'that outsize bundle of firewood', as she referred to the oak tree. She was quite glad to forget it, the felling and the unaccountably uncomfortable feeling it sometimes aroused in her. Sandel's return, and this new-found power were far more appealing. And, after all, it was only a game, really, she told herself. But the more she tasted power, the more appetizing it became. There was nothing quite like it for bucking one up. She could hardly wait for the moment when she would tell Sandel that she would 'probably definitely' abandon her tree-felling idea. She could already see the relief and gratitude shining on his face, as it used to shine, when he was little.

Just as she was about to speak, Sandel stood up.

Not wanting to endanger the atmosphere, he said, head bowed: 'I'm glad we spoke – about it.' And left the room, passing the thriving army of Bonsai specimens.

Alone in the passage, he felt stronger, fortified by their conversation. He decided he was now able to visit Mrs Fann, and he imagined the relief she would feel when he told her of his mother's reaction. But although he longed to see her, and make certain that *she*, the person he had met before she became disturbed, was still there, the thought of seeing her caused everything inside him to expand and turn upside down, until there was hardly any room left for him to breathe. He felt sick and hot. Forcing himself, he moved towards the back door.

In the lounge, Joy Perkins smiled to herself. It was lovely having Sandel back, well, present; the equivalent of turning on the central heating at the start of winter.

A few seconds later she heard the handle of the back door turning. He wasn't going out, to *that* woman, when the pie was almost ready? Her smile collapsed.

'Sandel!' she shouted, in the tone of a bus conductor. Then quickly she modulated her voice. 'Dinner'll soon be ready. It's a surprise! Again!' There was no answer. 'I haven't made that pie to decorate the kitchen.'

The door handle stopped turning.

After all, she justified herself to herself in the silence, she hadn't spent the morning slaving away at the stove for nothing, so she had no intention now of hiding her light under a bushel, or anything else for that matter.

Sandel smelt the pie, the promise of what lay beneath its crust being exhaled menacingly from the kitchen. The last thing he desired was food. He felt sated with emotion. All he could imagine consuming was cooled air. The thought of meat made him feel sick. Yet the idea (which he was unable to banish) of hurting and offending his mother hurt him even more. And the threat of her anger and another row was unbearable.

So they went into the kitchen and sat down. For a moment Joy thought that she had almost lost her appetite, too. But then seeing him sitting opposite her − a perfect couple, really, the younger man and the mature woman − renewed her hunger. She was, she thought, the perfect hostess.

Her guest swallowed with difficulty.

The following day, as Joy was dusting her lounge, she surveyed with pleasure the chairs Sandel and she had sat on the previous morning. She smoothed their cushions, gathering into her palms the last remnants of that pleasure. At tea-time, she decided, she would tell Sandel that she had given up the idea of felling the oak. After all, they needed some privacy from *that* particular neighbour.

As she straightened herself, a lorry drove into the Honourable's drive and then backed towards *her* bungalow. What did it think it was doing? She didn't like lorries or anything else trespassing on her property and crushing *her* gravel. She was just about to go out and express these emotions, when its engine was switched off. The back of the lorry was filled with harnesses, chains, chain-saws and saws, as if it were on its way to an abattoir. Three men wearing helmets, visors and ear muffs sat in the cabin. Joy rushed to fetch her long-distance glasses.

On the side of the lorry was written, 'Tree Fella's 'N Sons, Ltd. Tree Surgeons'. Were the sons the ones in the cabin? she wondered. She didn't often have so many men, *loose* in her drive. What an unexpected pleasure! Thank heavens she'd washed her doorstep in the nick of time, and still had the remains of a perm in her hair. She had no idea they were coming. She hadn't arranged anything, had she? She'd only written that letter. She hadn't signed anything official. As quickly as she could, she struggled out of her apron, becoming entangled in the apron strings. She put on a cardigan and, distractedly, snatched up a pair of gloves. Before any of the men pressed the doorbell, she dashed outside, closing the door silently behind her.

Through the keyhole Eileen screeched: 'Perky Perkins!'

I'll strangle that bird one day, she thought, stepping graciously, like the owner of a stately home, down her one front step.

At the same moment one of the men jumped down from the lorry.

'Good afternoon, madam. Are you Mrs Perkins, the lady of the 'ouse?'

'I am,' she acknowledged, wishing that he wouldn't speak so loudly, but enjoying the 'madam' and 'lady'. He was probably Mr Fella himself: a well-constructed looking man.

He nodded at the other men who jumped down, heavily, and joined him.

'Mr Flint, from the Council, confided in me that you might be wantin' a tree felled. So, as the boys and me was passin', I thought we'd just drop in and see the size of the beast.'

'Very kind, I'm sure.' Joy smiled what she considered was her 'sunrise' smile. The boys, who were sturdily dressed and booted, didn't smile back. Instead they kicked at the gravel with their metal-tipped boots.

'So where's the culprit, then?'

'Over there.' Joy Perkins nodded, to avoid pointing, and walked towards the tree, stepping superstitiously across the shadow of one of its branches. The boys followed. Quite an en-tou-rage, thought Joy, feeling almost bilingual. 'Your little helmets suit you very well, I must say,' she informed them flirtatiously, curiously (for her) unable to think of anything else to say. But she wanted them (and Sandel) to know (though how Sandel could, from this distance, she hadn't considered) that she was a man's woman and could manage men. Then she caught sight of the blank eye of his bedroom window and fervently hoped that he was not watching. Anyway, she wondered in panic, what was *she* doing out here, on the Honourable's lawn with these men? She didn't want the wretched tree cut down – really. And what would Sandel think? Suddenly he changed in her mind from being her little boy to being a grown up stranger: male.

Guiltily, she sidled round the tree's girth. The boys followed. Stocky as tree trunks they were, and a bit oppressive – like the weather. She almost felt she was in a forest, of men. If only she could extract a smile from one of them she'd feel better, and less naked, standing on her neighbour's lawn. But probably, she decided, their work made them serious.

'Get the measure then, Slasher.'

What a name! giggled Joy to herself, attempting to lighten it. Slasher wore orange ear muffs and a battered black helmet from which lots of hair fanned out, of the colour and length of Jane Russell's, in one of her early films. But there the resemblance ended. From deep inside his chest pocket he produced a measuring tape. Joy Perkins was suddenly aware that she was now in full view of Mrs Fann's bedroom window. Sweat began to trickle, independently of her, it felt, down her back. With her high heels sinking into the grass, she crept still further round the tree.

'I was thinking . . .' She commenced, moving her hand away from the bark of the tree which had been supporting her, while imprinting itself deep into her palm. 'I was thinking of not having it fell . . .'

'Pretty big job, ain't it, Bud?' Mr Fella, or whatever his ridiculous name was, rudely interrupted her.

Bud's small face gazed up calculatingly at the gigantic spread of leaves above him.

'Tis if we makes a mistake. There's some tonnage of wood-flesh there. And the 'ouses is pretty close.' He looked at both houses, accosting them with his gaze. 'Wouldn't like to see this fallin' the wrong way!' He laughed, joined by the others.

'Might 'ave to do quite a bit of tidyin' up if it did,' joked Slasher, obviously the wit of the party.

Mr Fella moved to the centre of the lawn.

'That's your bungalow, is it?' he asked.

'Yes, as I said. My son's and mine.' The word 'son' strengthened and then weakened her.

Slasher and Bud removed half-smoked cigarettes from behind their small ears and with deft casual movements ignited matches on their skin-tight jeaned thighs which apparently contained stored-up fire. Their cigarettes glowing, they looked steadily at her.

'As I was saying . . .' Mrs Perkins's usually authoritative voice was absorbed by the density of the tree, while her stature appeared to diminish in size, the longer she was surrounded by the men.

'Beg your pardon?'

Is he deaf? Joy wondered, distraught. Can't be much good to have a deaf tree-feller. She knew that he had sensed something wavering in her, and that his immovable stance was trying to drag her into the centre of the lawn.

'We was thinking,' she enunciated clearly, for his sake, while exhausting herself. What did he think she was? A speech therapist? Why couldn't he move towards her? 'We was thinking it would be better to leave the tree here. For the moment.'

'Well p'raps you coulda let us know that when we arrived, instead of 'alf-way fru the job.' Mr Fella turned on his metal-tipped heel. 'Come on, lads. The lady don't seem to know 'er own mind – eh, Slash?'

Slasher looked too bored to respond.

The lads clanked back into the lorry cabin which was also studded, causing their boots to scrape and spark. Bud revved up the engine, its huge aggressive roar filling both gardens. With a crushing and spurting of gravel, they drove away.

Joy stood, stranded, beneath the great tree whose shadow appeared to lengthen and thicken every second. She raised a gloved hand to her mouth and nibbled distractedly at its loose cotton threads, feeling like a rabbit caught in the spotlights from the two windows.

She wished she could burrow her way back to her bungalow and discover that the whole incident had been imagined. But she couldn't. She was separated from her front door by her thirty-foot garden – acres it felt – above which a storm was brewing.

From their two rooms, Constance Fann and Sandel Perkins had observed this scene.

Constance Fann moved away from her bedroom window. The lorry had disappeared, but left behind, in her head, was the clink and jangle of the harness tightening round the trunk, and the hoarse roar and animal whine of the chain saw tearing its way into the flesh of the tree. The torture was mounting inside her.

She ran downstairs.

Into the samphire pram she put her portable wireless, and then walked towards the road, walking with such power that the upper part of her body seemed suspended on her moving hips. *The whole earth is tied up, bound with black ribbons of roads. Soon I will not be able to get out. All the trees will be ground down into stumps. Everything will be asphalted and concreted over and I won't be able to breathe.*

Church bells started to ring, the great oval sounds falling and breaking on the ground, littering the pavements. *They should sweep them up. Immediately.* She could feel a frown stretching all through her, reaching to her finger tips. She switched on her wireless and thousands of harpsichord notes overflowed from the pram.

When she reached the village, she entered a shop. She wanted to speak. But the words had no sound. The only sound which came from her was — from her hand, which held the aluminium door handle, hissing and sparking with static electricity.

'Mrs Fann? Madam?' she heard dimly and then loudly. The sounds were mounting and she was crumbling. She left the shop.

It was safer, more prudent, to walk in the middle of the road. On the pavement, objects could fall from above. Bars of metal from houses being constructed could fall with increasing velocity until they reached and killed her. The fish-stall could capsize and she would be buried beneath great girths of turbot.

At the end of the village she opened a gate and started to walk through a field, pushing the pram. Through the airless evening she waded, labouring across the sea-like field. She stopped. In front of her was an elm tree. Ivy was mounting and shrouding it. *Ivy will mount me; its tendrils will cling, its dark leaves will creep over my face, entering my mouth until I am all green.* She moved quickly away. From the pram, fortissimo music flowed, squeezing her between cymbals and drum beats.

She left the pram and started to run, running until she reached a dip in the field. And there, below her, behind shrubs and tall grasses, were railway lines: the cold steel glinted at her. Enticing. Closer towards the lines she walked, the blood in her veins pulled by the hidden electricity. She stood on the solid sleepers and bent towards them, listening. The lines started to tingle, alive and expectant to an approaching train: a clot racing along the arteries. She moved closer, absorbed. Then she saw the train – a dot in the distance. The tingling in the lines intensified. If she gripped them, the approaching thundering would enter her and she would be filled with all the secretly flowing electricity: the passion of its forward surging.

But the noise was becoming unbearable. She would be destroyed by noise.

She pulled herself up the other side of the bank as the train whipped past, its speed and sound assaulting her. It was raping the silence, murdering the ground.

On she walked, walking until finally she reached the back of her garden. Someone had lit a bonfire. *I shall wrap myself up in its smoke.*

Bound in smoke, she entered her house, and returned to her bedroom, and the safety of the darkness behind her closed eyes. But she could not sleep. It was too hot, and it was becoming hotter. The heat was knocking into her forehead.

Through her bedroom window came the smell of over-ripe apples, from the loaded, painfully swaying apple trees. The apples rubbed and bruised together in the heavy evening air; their scent was so strong she could taste it — breath from another mouth. With her foot she stretched and tried to close the curtains. But they swung open again, the clammy blue-palmed hands of the night pressing against the window panes. Then she saw the moon, manoeuvring itself to peer and shine between the curtains — and the oak tree, which was awesome and dark. She closed her eyes, blocking it out.

As she lay there, her hair on the pillow looked dry. And from her and the vermilion sheets rose a smell of bonfire smoke, as though she were slowly smouldering.

While the huge presence of the tree-felling lorry had filled their garden, Sandel had rushed from his bedroom to the front door, his thoughts racing to left and right. Should he go first to Mrs Fann, or to his mother and those men? He didn't know. All he knew was that he would have liked to trample the whole lot of them into the ground.

'I can't live here any more,' he had said aloud, and returned to his bedroom. With the minimum of thought he had started to clear his room, his blind hands snatching at his belongings. The pile of possessions which he intended to incinerate grew in size minute by minute.

As he moved about his room, he had still been able to taste the meal his mother had prepared for him on the previous day, the combination of it, and her deceit over the tree-felling, having turned his sickness to fury. How *could* she do this? he had asked himself over and over again. 'She's *supposed* to be my mother!' he had said aloud, flinging the sentence into the room. His thoughts raced like a forest fire from recollection to recollection.

When the lorry had finally roared out of the drive, he had taken an armful of belongings into the garden. Kneeling beside the incinerator, he ignited it with old photographs of Serissa Foetida and himself. The photographs jumped into flame, causing him to move backwards, and straighten himself.

'What am I *doing* here? With this bonfire?' he shouted at himself. While the flames bit and snapped at the hot air, he rushed towards Mrs Fann's front door. But there had been no answer to his knocking, the knocks just landing in the empty house. Where *was* she? As he turned to go, he noticed that the samphire pram was missing. Perhaps she hadn't seen the lorry – and was better – and was gathering samphire. Unsuccessfully he had attempted to breathe life into his thoughts.

In panic, he ran towards the main road, not knowing which way to turn. So he ran towards the village. But the streets were empty of prams or people. He ran on, feeling the air passing him, the pavement deadening his steps. Where the village ended and the fields started, a gate stood open, through which he felt himself pulled. On the rim of the field stood the curved outline of the pram. He ran faster, the long grasses like nooses around his ankles. But when he reached it the pram had been empty, except for a portable wireless from whose almost dead batteries had come the slowly expiring notes of flute music. He looked around. Below the pram, in a hollow, there were railway lines. Barely breathing he gazed down unbelievingly at the gleaming steel, forcing himself to look from left to right, his white face cold in the heat. The innocent lines continued undisturbed, but in league, towards infinity.

He had rushed back to the pram and battled with it across

the bumpy field. Dragging it behind him to make it look less pram-like, he pulled it through the deserted village whose shop windows felt full of eyes. As he had continued pulling it, the great bulky conveyance kept snapping at his heels. So he pushed it forwards, feeling even more foolish, like some single-parent family.

With relief he had turned off the main road and walked towards Mrs Fann's house.

In a downstairs window, a light went on. He stopped, and breathed again, after what felt like hours of surviving on one breath.

She was downstairs. So she *must* be better.

As he had stood, surrounded by the dusk, and gazed at the hot light from her window, all alternative thoughts withdrew and faded. All he could imagine was her loveliness (and that happiness he had seen in her garden.) His blood seemed to grow heavier and darker as it pulsed deeply and steadily through his veins. His breathing became quicker until he felt there was hardly any breath left in his body (or in the air around him) to breathe. He felt he would expire with longing.

Then the light in her window went out.

Almost roughly he pulled himself away from the blackened house and walked slowly towards the bungalow.

From his mother's bedroom window a subdued green-tinted light had leaked – more like darkness than light. But, despite its timidity, it succeeded in seeping into his conscience. Painfully he had tried to stop himself imagining his mother sitting alone in her room, with only her aloneness as company. Her loneliness weighed upon him more heavily than if it were his own. And in some strange way his mother (alone in her room and oblivious of what he was feeling) *still* managed to intrude and eavesdrop on his desire, making him feel angry and embarrassed. He turned away from the bungalow.

The bonfire had still been burning. He went and stood next to it, scorching himself in the hot thundery night.

Downstairs, in Constance Fann's house, the air had been so hot that if, she thought, she put her thermometer into the mouth of the night the mercury would have risen and overflowed into her damp palm. After fetching the thermometer, she carefully broke the bud from its stem, holding her hand out to catch the mysterious quicksilver balls, her tongue longing to taste the untouchable liquid. But, as she raised her hand to her mouth, the mercury had raced over her palm and been swallowed by the carpet.

She had switched off the light and returned to her bed, the weight of the night heat heavy as a body on her.

Outside her window, the great blackened trunk and spreading branches of the oak tree were solid and unmoving, until a stray breeze entered the tree and there was a stirring of leaves, a heaving, as of someone turning over in sleep.

A few minutes later, the force of its blackness and strength pulled her from her bed.

Into the garden she wandered, where the night was so thick it could have been sliced.

Towards the comfort of the oak she moved, her hot forehead pressed against the about-to-thunder air. On the grass the shadow of the tree was stretched out. She lay down, her face in the grass. *I shall roll myself up in its long shadow, roll to the heart of the tree where the shadow is stored, and where I will be imbued with the tree's bull-like strength.* On a smooth mound of turf she lay, its greenness pressed to her lips, its scent filling her mouth. Her body was sealed to the green beating heart of the ground. *I shall mould the lover of the earth into my body and be infused with the rush of its green sap.*

Beside the bonfire Sandel stood and watched, knowing that he should not be watching. In his hand he held a palmful of jasmine, still attached to its branch, his hand full of scent. She is *not* better, he told himself fiercely, wishing he could instantly dismantle and smash the great edifice of his desire, inside which he suddenly felt acutely lonely. It was useless and ridiculous. It was because of *her* that he had built up this phantom. And now she had deserted him. And perhaps . . . the words his mother had spoken about her 'having it off' forced themselves into his mind. But he couldn't bear to think about them. They weren't true. He wanted to crush the hateful sentence. Without his being aware of it, his hand crushed the jasmine.

The storm moved closer; the brightness of the lightning intensified as it exercised in the sky, kindling the heavy dry air.

Constance Fann rose from the ground. Quickly she walked to her studio. Sandel followed, slowly, from a distance.

From her sculpture she removed the damp cloths. *I shall smash it; trample the clay back into the earth where it belongs.* She raised her hand.

'Please don't. Don't destroy it.'

Sandel pleaded, wondering how, minutes ago, he could have accused her for what he felt and what his mother had insinuated. The combination of his accusation and her anguish was unbearable.

'It's your *work*.'

He spoke again, from the blackened doorway, not daring to approach further, fearing his body might ignite of itself, with desire.

Constance Fann turned and looked at him: at the sweetness and concern on his young man's face. She continued to look. She hadn't seen a face for a long time, it seemed, though whose face it was she was uncertain. But its kindness she dimly recognized – in some far-off part of herself.

After a few more minutes, she placed her hand tentatively on her sculpture, before slowly covering it with the damp cloths.

Sandel sat in his mother's white kitchen, while outside flashes of even whiter lightning whipped at the walls of the low-crouching bungalow.

At one moment, in the studio, he had thought that Mrs Fann was going to recognize him, break through the mist of her confusion, and even smile. But there had been no recognition or reflection of him in her large eyes, in which she, too, seemed partly absent. He wasn't even on the rim of her consciousness, he told himself, adamantly, trying to force himself to listen. The sorrow he felt for her anguish made him ache, almost physically.

Yet apparently he could do nothing for her. But where had all her happiness and strength gone? Or had he just imagined it? Round and round his thoughts revolved, making him feel dizzy, until he wanted to yell out: 'Stop!'

He stood up, abruptly, knowing that what had happened to Mrs Fann had been caused by his mother's relentless pruning of life. It was she who had destroyed Constance Fann's happiness. And perhaps she would destroy him, too; though this he could barely contemplate. He felt he would like to cut, sever for ever, the hateful umbilical cord which bound him to her. Surely, he thought wildly they could invent some other way to be born!

On the draining board was his mother's Bonsai pruning knife. He gripped it, its handle filling his clenched fist. At the same moment a great breath of outside air was breathed into the room by the open kitchen window, sucking in the curtain. Inhaling this breath, he rushed down the passage. Above him, thunder started to rumble, stumbling over itself as it tumbled out of the sky. For a moment he leant against his mother's closed bedroom door, and then ran into the lounge.

From the windowsill he seized the Bonsai trees. One by one he pulled the crippled plants from their midget containers and then cut their stems, putting an end to their deformed lives. Then he flung the knife into the passage, as far as his energy would take it.

Into a suitcase he threw most of his belongings, moving round his room as quickly as he could before his decision to leave had time to waver. Although he knew that he could no longer bear to go on living in the bungalow with his mother, each movement he made to leave it, he had to force forward.

A quarter of an hour later, he carried his half-empty suitcase from his room and walked out of the bungalow into the dawn, slamming the door behind him, as he had been told *not* to do, over and over again.

He looked at the garden surrounding him; it felt alien, as though it suddenly belonged to someone else, not his mother. He walked towards the road, unable even to glance out of the corner of his eye at Constance Fann's house, though he could feel the power of it pulling at the tendons in his neck. As the memory of her distress surged towards him again, he knew that he had to remove his desire and demolish it.

The proximity of her distress and his desire were hateful to him. But at the same time he was aware that nothing could remove what he had glimpsed in her: her happiness – her joy. Some part of her had already taken root inside him. Was this the *something* that other people called love? It felt like love – even though (to his shame) he realized that he didn't really know what love felt like. For a moment he wished there was someone he could ask. But then he knew that he didn't need to ask: it was so.

Although he hated to admit that, the last time he had seen her, she hadn't recognized him, something about the way she had laid her hand on her sculpture – however tentatively – made him certain that she would recover. Her work and her happiness would restore her. He could not do that, he acknowledged sadly.

It started to rain; the first drops warm as sweat on his skin. At the bus stop, he leant against the straightness of a lamp-post, his face streaming with water.

When the bus drew up, he boarded it, not looking at its destination. Onto the rack he heaved his half-empty suitcase, which felt heavy and bulky with ... He didn't know what, until the weight of his pain shifted inside him, and the bus moved. *I am being removed by force from this place*, he told himself, *being taken away by this anonymous machine.*

Sitting alone, surrounded by the empty rattling bus, the rough unfamiliar material of the seat beneath him, he wondered where he would go to. He would go as far as the bus would take him, and then decide. And should he buy a single ticket or a return?

'Yes?' enquired the bus conductor. Waiting.

'To the terminus. Please.'

'Single?'

'Yes.' His hand felt weak as it took the ticket. But the decision had been made for him. Perhaps, he thought unexpectedly, he would visit his father. The thought startled him. But then, in his empty hand, he felt the memory of the stone, comforting and strong. Yes, he decided, he would go and see his father.

As his mother's bungalow and Constance Fann's house came rapidly into view, from inside the safety of the bus, his head turned involuntarily. Gripping his single-fare ticket, he faced the two houses, looking at them intently until they were out of sight – removed by the bus. And at that moment he knew that the cord which attached him to those two houses could not, probably, be broken by time or distance: it had infinite elasticity. But how far would he have to go, and for how long, before he could return, restored?

As soon as Joy thought it was 'all-clear', she opened her bedroom door an inch and peered out. Cautiously she ventured into the dim passage, and then tripped. She looked down. At her feet was her Bonsai pruning knife, its glinting steel the only light.

'Why can't he put things back where they belong?' she heard herself exclaim, her words needing the reassurance of their own sound. Not daring to touch the knife, she pushed it with her foot against the skirting board, and went into the lounge.

Her hands flew up to her mouth. It looked as if a whirlwind had spent the night in there. She slumped down on her knees and, small and suddenly withered-looking, sat amongst the battered plants. They had all been vandalized. Even Serissa Foetida, which was almost the same age as Sandel. And she had always assumed that after she had 'passed over', Sandel would look after the plants, and her memory at the same time, thus extending her life. She touched Serissa's oozing trunk, and with disgust withdrew her finger, smelling the foetid odour for the first time.

As she continued to sit, stunned and wilted, amidst the scattered dwarf trunks and branches, she began to feel a quite unexpected relief at the removal of the burden of something cherished. Her passion for her plants seemed to have been wiped out with the same stroke which had destroyed them. She didn't want plants now. She wanted Sandel, even though he had murdered her treasures.

Back down the passage she went to his bedroom. She knocked, just in case some part of him remained to answer. The room appeared to have expanded during the night, its emptiness occupied by the beginnings of an echo. *Where were his things?* Quickly she left, closing the door behind her to shut out the sight.

But where was she to go? The emptiness of Sandel's room was starting to creep through the bungalow.

She went into the concealed kitchen.

'Where's Sandel?' she almost sobbed, knowing he was nowhere near. 'Where did I go wrong with him?' she asked pleadingly, in a minute voice.

'Pardon?' Eileen, whose existence she had forgotten, commented in a muffled voice from her still-covered cage. Joy didn't hear her. *What does Sandel think of me?* The question made her shudder. *I didn't ask those blasted Tree Fellas to come. But he thinks I did.* The unfairness of the misunderstanding clung tenaciously and uncomfortably to her.

'What am I going to *do*?' She overheard herself speaking again. There didn't seem to be anything to *do*. But *where* was Sandel, so early in the morning? And it was Sunday, too. Still Sunday. Perhaps, she thought with a rush of hope, he's at the big house, with the Honourable. She didn't care where he was as long as he was somewhere – near.

Without bothering to look into her compact-mirror, she dabbed her nose nervously with a powder puff and wiped a scar of lipstick across her mouth. Then she grabbed her handbag and, summoning as much courage as she could, left the house.

As she walked quickly up her neighbour's drive, her body felt it was being watched on all sides.

Before she reached the front door, it was opened. She

stepped back, shocked. It had been quite some time since she had seen Mrs Fann. Where had all her irritating happiness gone? Where . . .? Mrs Fann appeared almost as vacant as Sandel's room.

'I've mislaid Sandel. D'you know where he is – please?' The words rushed out of her mouth.

'Sandel?' Constance Fann pronounced the word as though it was the first she had spoken for a long time. 'Sandel? Dear boy.' His name, and the sweetness of his concern, moved fractionally towards each other.

'Yes, he's a nice boy, my boy is,' Joy acknowledged proudly, reclaiming him, while trying to ignore the tremors of her guilt. Sandel obviously wasn't here with the Honourable, so what was the point of staying? But she found she was unable to move from her spot on the doorstep: Mrs Fann's distressed expression immobilized and silenced her. Still, she consoled herself, it wasn't her fault that that wretched lorry had driven into her drive. She hadn't asked it to come. She'd decided against the felling. She'd had enough dealings with plants to last her a lifetime. All that fuss over a tree – a bit of hardwood – anyone would think it was human! Surely it wasn't that which had made her go strange . . . and . . . *Oh shut up!* she said to herself. Even she, occasionally, found her inner chattering exhausting. Mrs Fann was still looking at her.

From her handbag, Joy Perkins took a scrap of paper and her biro. In small unsteady letters she wrote:

'*The oak tree won't be coming down. Afteral.*'

Above her, she felt Mrs Fann's presence.

'*Sorry for the trouble,*' she added, the letters coming as reluctantly from her, as the ink from her near-empty biro. She handed the note to Mrs Fann.

Constance Fann looked at her, and then smiled: a quiet smile.

Joy Perkins felt confused. She didn't know what to do

with the smile. She turned round and walked away, not daring to look back.

As though entering icy water, she went quickly into Sandel's room again. It was still empty of him. So she started to tidy and dust what little there was to be tidied. When she had finished she stepped back and surveyed it. The room looked as it had before she had started.

'I can't live here on my own, can I? It's not natural,' she conferred with her duster. 'Well I won't have to, will I? He'll be back shortly. Probably tonight.'

Without warning or invitation, she heard again Mrs Fann's voice speaking Sandel's name. More motherly it had been, really, than what she'd imagined. *But I'm his mother, and one's enough.* She clamped down on any further thoughts, and went into the lounge. Dawn was sitting curled up on Sidney's chair.

'Get off of there!' She clapped her hands. Dawn stayed where she was. 'She's gone deaf,' Joy confided in herself. She lifted Dawn onto her lap and, unaware of what she was doing, sat down on Sidney's chair. 'Our Sandel will be back tonight. Probably,' she informed the cat, a question mark hovering at the end of her sentence. Finding Dawn's powers of communication limited, and the silence in the room unnerving, she got up, fetched a pad of writing paper and started to write a letter.

Dear Sidney, she began, and then stopped. And re-membered. Sidney had been a thorn in her flesh all right, from day one – well, day two – but a thorn she couldn't do without. That was, until Sandel, her 'little man' had arrived, and Sidney had somehow become redundant in their life. But now things were different. Perhaps he'd changed, grown less difficult and would need the companionship of a mature woman. He was probably lonely, poor thing. She picked up her biro again, but as she did so, she felt a dart of pain in her body, in the same place in her stomach where she had felt it before.

'But it'll pass,' she told Dawn, in her indomitable little voice.

She put down her biro, and sat still. A few seconds later, that quiet smile of Mrs Fann's sailed into her mind. Why? she wondered.

Constance Fann sat in her studio. Several days had passed. She looked down at the scrap of paper which Mrs Perkins had handed to her and re-read the words scribbled on it. Although she still seemed to be reading them and their meaning through water, this time they remained where they were, facing her in black: '*The oak tree won't be coming down. Afteral.*' She looked out and up at the tree.

It stood, powerful and still, filling her eyes.

She remembered having watched Mrs Perkins until she had disappeared into her bungalow. How small she was – tenacious when facing one, yet battered from behind. She read the last sentence again. '*Sorry for the trouble.*' Slowly there floated up from her memory Mrs Perkins's disturbing smile, to be replaced by her greater look of anxiety. As Constance Fann recalled the hurriedly made-up face, and imagined the courage she must have had to accumulate to come and see her, she was reminded of a gutted house, which has been hastily and cheaply renovated, to hide the inner deterioration.

Is she, perhaps, ill?

'And Sandel is her son?' she said aloud to herself. Slowly his name and his concern for her fused together, causing what felt like a bandaging of her heart. *One day I shall thank him. And one day, perhaps, I shall ask if I can sculpt him, and his kindness.* But how, she wondered, would she persuade the clay to convey kindness? Where, apart from the eyes, and perhaps the hands, is it revealed in the body?

The question was suddenly absorbing and intriguing.

Unable to wait, she stood up and carefully removed the cloths from the clay torso. She stepped back to look at it, fearful at what this first glance might reveal. Slowly she revolved it round on its stand. As she did so, to her relief, she discovered that what she saw was not so much alarming as strange. Strange, because it was not quite as she had imagined it would be. There appeared to be another element in it which she had not planned in her original conception of it. But what was it? It was not displeasing – more surprising. She looked at it for several minutes, puzzled, as she continued to turn it, until the back was facing her. There was something in the slight stoop of the shoulders which reminded her of someone. But who was it? She hadn't been thinking of anyone in particular while she had worked.

Then she knew who it was. It was Sandel Perkins. It was not something about him which was instantly recognizable; it was just an aspect of him, more something which would be seen in a glance, out of the corner of the eye. It disappeared if she concentrated on it. But how very strange that it was there at all. That unbeknown to her this particular (and perhaps most touching) side of him had entered her hands, entered the clay.

She stretched out on a chaise-longue, close to the window.

'I think I can work again,' she said aloud to herself. 'Perhaps I *will* be able to finish the commission in time.'

A short while later, across her outstretched feet, the shadow of a bird flew, on its way to perch in the oak tree. She bent forward to touch the shadow. It had disappeared. But left behind was a mysterious happiness.

The Holiday

This year they were going to be three for the holiday: Pru; her small son, Clive-Robert; and a friend's young daughter, Vicky. During the weekend, however, there would be four of them. Pru's husband, Charles, would be present.

Last year they had rented a bungalow on the coast, the flat grey waveless coast which Pru said she loved so much. Between that year and this, the bungalow had been washed away. There had been gale warnings. But no one had quite believed them: that the flat grey waveless sea would ever do such a thing. This year they were staying further inland. But the sea could still be heard.

Last year there had been three more of them for the holiday: Vicky's mother; Pru's elder son, Rody; and of course Charles, who had stayed for the whole week – last year.

Vicky, who was eleven and a half and an only child, and her mother had shared a room (her father, after separating from her mother three-and-a-half years ago, having died). Vicky had settled herself happily into the sensation of being surrounded by and almost a part of a real family. She considered that Rody was her real friend, even though he was three years older than she. Too old now, she presumed, for holidays by the sea. So she was glad he had a younger brother. In fact, when she had been told that Clive-Robert was 'on the way', she had been very excited, almost as if she were going to have a baby brother. And that's what he had *felt* like last year, too, when he was six.

Vicky's mother thought it would be beneficial for her daughter to spend a little time away from her, and to have some male companionship, even though Clive-Robert was younger and Charles could only come for part of the time. (Pru had indicated, briefly, that he could only manage weekends . . . these days.) So Vicky assumed that she had been invited as a companion for Pru as well as for Clive-Robert. This dual rôle made her feel expansive and grown-up, and she had hardly been able to wait for the holiday to begin. For a few days she would have Charles as a father and Clive-Robert as a brother – not that she was ever quite certain what fathers or brothers were supposed to be like.

As Vicky sat opposite Clive-Robert, eating her first holiday breakfast, she noticed that this year he was thinner, had cold-looking knees, a blazer which smelt of different soups and a highish, educated-sort-of voice, even though he hadn't been educated for long. Although he resembled Rody, his eyes were cooler and paler, and kept looking at her. But, she reassured herself, he *was* Rody's brother. (When he was a baby she had helped to change his triangular nappies, holding the big pink safety-pins in her mouth.) Also, he was so much smaller than Rody, his smallness causing her to stoop when walking with him. But she enjoyed stooping. It made *her* feel motherly, and *him* feel brotherly.

After breakfast, Vicky helped Pru make jam tarts for tea, by which time Charles would have arrived. The tarts were filled with red ponds of jam which matched the dashes of red Pru often wore and were somehow theatrical. (Pru had been on the stage.) Charles wore dark city suits, even on holiday. Vicky thought that the serious London clothes made him appear as though he were leaving, or had never quite arrived. Even when he removed his tie and unbuttoned his top shirt button he still didn't look 'on holiday'. So she preferred it when he kept the button buttoned. However, when she and her mother stayed with Pru and Charles for weekends in London, it was from the dark pockets of these city suits that Charles had produced bags of marshmallows, after returning from the Christian Scientists' meetings. That such sweets should emerge from such darkness, after attending the Christian Scientists, had astonished Vicky.

Now she enjoyed being alone with Pru, talking and laughing in a womanly way in the steaming kitchen. It was becoming almost like last year, when the bungalow had been filled with the word 'darling', to-ing and fro-ing between Charles and Pru; also laughter, especially Pru's laughter, because Pru, having been an actress, had taken lessons in elocution, and so knew how to laugh. Unlike last year, though, this year Vicky had her *own* bedroom, next to Clive-Robert's.

After lunch they set off to meet Charles. Beside a windy bus stop they waited, resolutely, the sea air filling their mouths. Charles was not on the first bus. Pru and Clive-Robert started to stamp their feet as people do when it is cold, Clive-Robert stamping double-time, even though it was not cold. It was midsummer. But Vicky knew that she would have waited for ever for a father, even at a windy bus stop.

When Charles finally arrived, Vicky, from a discreet distance, watched the others being embraced, and then felt her own shoulder being patted, while Clive-Robert watched. They walked back to the bungalow, spread out in a line across the narrow road, causing Vicky nearly to slip into a ditch while trying to keep her place.

When they arrived back, the bungalow echoed, intermittently, with 'darling' being called from room to room, chiefly by Pru.

Clive-Robert and Charles then disappeared. Vicky didn't go and search for them because she had been told that they were 'great friends', and wouldn't want to be disturbed. So she just waited, wondering what to do with the awkward-shaped piece of time.

Later, Pru, glancing at Vicky as though she had forgotten she was there, suggested that Charles needed a rest and that Vicky and Clive-Robert might like to go to the beach and play.

So down to the sea they went, he walking silently ahead. Along a prickly path they walked, the sides of which scratched their legs, while the sharp wind sliced at the edges of their cheeks. Clive-Robert decided they would make a huge hole in the sand.

Vicky wondered why they couldn't make a sand-boat as she and Rody had done last year. But Clive-Robert, standing rigid with the wind buffeting at him, said he wasn't interested in boats, this year. As he was younger, Vicky let him have his way. And together they started to shovel and dig while the sand slipped and slid, soon reaching up to their armpits. Vicky loved embracing huge armfuls of sand, and felt happy.

Finally the hole was large enough for them to sit in, submerged. But Vicky's hair could still be seen above the ground, blowing like a little danger flag on the dunes.

'Daddy might stay for the whole week, like last year!' Clive-Robert said suddenly, filling the hole with his hopeful sentence.

'I thought he was staying only for the weekend,' Vicky commented.

'Well, he might. And he might not,' Clive-Robert, confused, almost shouted at Vicky, who was not deaf.

After a considerable pause, he asked, 'Why doesn't your father come for the weekend?'

'Because he's busy,' Vicky felt compelled, unwillingly, to

answer, while digging with her heel to nowhere in particular.

'You're spoiling the floor,' Clive-Robert reminded her. And then asked in his high, educated-sort-of voice, 'Why is he busy at *weekends*? Most fathers aren't.'

'Well . . . he used to come,' Vicky said hesitatingly. '*Long* before you were born,' she added, quickly summoning her three-and-a-half years' seniority. 'But now he's *very* busy,' she concluded vehemently.

The silence in the hole began to prickle and move infinitesimally, like the sand surrounding them.

'I think he's dead,' Clive-Robert said slowly but decisively.

'He's *not*!' Vicky exclaimed with conviction, though her voice lacked volume, as if it had been sucked in by the damp, porous walls.

'Mummy says he is,' Clive-Robert continued in a smallish but persistent tone.

In the khaki-coloured light of the hole, Vicky saw that Clive-Robert's white face was now bearded with sand. What might have been a small smile hovered across it. She felt shrivelled. She hated Clive-Robert, and stood up. Her face, above ground, was slapped by the rough salty wind. Standing over him she noticed how little he was, sitting hunched in the hole. She wanted to break up his stick-like thinness, kick the walls in and cause a landslide on top of him. In her hand she held a palmful of sand which, while she gripped it, sieved slowly away.

'You're hurting the walls,' Clive-Robert reminded her again.

Vicky didn't answer, and with one step climbed out of the hole, feeling its sides slipping under her towards him. Quickly she walked away.

'Hey! . . . We haven't finished playing . . .' Clive-Robert called after her.

But Vicky had already gone. Her feet were being tripped up by snares of grass as she stumbled forwards, her forehead pressed towards the bungalow. Then she remembered that it was to Pru and Charles she was heading. And she longed more than anything to be running towards her own mother. She didn't want to stay here any more. But there were still five more days, the rest of this day and all the nights. Time stretched in front of her as endlessly as the flat grey beach whose rim she couldn't see. Then she thought she heard Clive-Robert's plimsolled feet thudding behind her, and she walked faster.

In the bungalow, Pru and Charles were having tea, sitting at opposite ends of the table, as though they were in a tea-shop.

'You look rather windblown, Vicky,' Pru said, extra kindly, and offered her one of the red-pond tarts which Vicky took but couldn't eat. It blocked her throat. She longed to tell Pru what had happened but knew she could not because Pru was Clive-Robert's mother.

And because what he had said was true.

'Where's old Clive-Robert? Is he coming?' Charles asked.

Vicky nodded, feeling stiff.

'I have to leave a day earlier than I'd anticipated, I'm afraid. So I want to see as much of him as possible. I've brought him a dressing-gown,' he added, concluding his speech-like sentences, while securing his top button which was already secure. Pru didn't seem to be listening, and offered Vicky a second tart, the first uneaten one apparently invisible to her.

A little later Clive-Robert came in looking sulphur-coloured with sand stuck to him. Vicky avoided facing him, feeling that with the slightest raising of her eyes he might catch her look and renew his attack. She wished that he would be made to go to bed early. But instead, after he'd been given his present and informed of his father's early departure, he was allowed to stay up late, dressed in his boy's dressing-gown which was too big for him, Vicky noticed with satisfaction.

Clive-Robert played quietly in a corner by himself, every now and then looking up at his father, while his dressing-gown appeared to increase in size until he was almost lost inside it.

That night, when they had all gone to bed, the door of Pru's and Charles's bedroom seemed extra thick, and firmly closed.

From her bed, Vicky's still-white face peered out into the blackness. She felt the rented sheet on top of her; and she tried not to think of Clive-Robert next door. But the walls of her room seemed to have become porous, and she couldn't stop him, or the sight of him lost in his dressing-gown, seeping through.

She longed for the holiday to end, and willed the night forwards. But the night plodded stubbornly on, at its own pace.

The Butcher's
Christmas Story

In the early morning the butcher opened the door of his shop and while it was still wrapped in fog as thick and white as bandages, he raised the blinds which the evening before he had pulled down at six p.m., like tired eyelids, closing the red eyes of the shop. Then he wiped the iced windows – like bathing a glass patient. While he squeezed his chamois leather cloth with warm soapy water, he looked at his window – at the chickens which hung upside down, their eyes closed.

Today was Christmas Eve, his favourite and busiest time of year, when he would spend hours, before opening, arranging the window. On the left side, he placed trays of the palest pink meat, starting with the large calves' livers; he always thought it strange that such 'little fellas' should have such large livers. He loved the sheen on liver and heart, its pretty colours reminding him of a puddle when oil is spilt on it. Next came the trays of the slightly darker pink of veal fillet which (at today's price) he handled as gently as a baby – unless a customer wanted an escalope, when he would beat it as thin as a net curtain. Through the spectrum of pinks and reds he worked, from veal to pork to lamb to beef, until he reached the maroons and browns of the hearts and kidneys; weird internal colours they were, he thought, wondering why they were so dark.

He stepped back and proudly surveyed the display. But as

usual he was confronted by a dilemma: whether to put all the livers, hearts and kidneys together or (as he was doing now) arrange them according to colour? It was the artist in him, his wife Doreen said, when he would smile modestly, his autumnal-coloured moustache stretching from ear to ear, like a furry smile. Above his worn chopping block, of which he was proud, he had hung what he considered to be an Old Master: a large poster which announced 'Great Grass Makes Great Beef. Irish Beef', depicting sunny emerald Irish fields with a chopping block in the centre of them – not cattle as one would expect; it was the subtlety of it that he appreciated.

Doreen was also an artist in her own right, 'an artiste in paarzley' he called her (pronouncing parsley as if it had several a's and a z). In fact it was Doreen who had made the breakthrough from plastic to fresh parsley, and now did all the finer display work, like sticking little sprigs into the sides of the pigs' mouths, which made them look like farmers sucking straw. Doreen had a great sense of humour, too.

At that moment, reflected in the window, he thought he saw Doreen. Or was it her? There was such a lot of bright colour in his shop that he couldn't be certain. This was because Doreen always wore red – at least reds – and had high colouring, so there was a continual battle before his eyes as all the different reds fought together. It *was* Doreen.

'Cooee! Ronald! I'm just off for a bit of shopping,' she called. She got onto her bicycle and cycled away fast down the hill, her mac flying out, making her look like some giant bird flying low over the road. She had on her leather boots, he noticed, which reached right up to her knees and still continued on up.

The butcher had built his wife a little glass cage in his shop behind which she sat and smiled and took the money. When they were first married, he had polished the glass each morning; he enjoyed 'polishing up' Doreen. Now Doreen polished it herself. As well as the polishing and the 'paarzley' display, she also used to do the final plucking of the turkeys at Christmas, plucking them until they were almost as smooth as her own skin. But she always left a few feathers on the turkeys' ankles; they looked less naked, rather like cancan dancers. She didn't like Ronald doing these more feminine things (like the lattice-work fat on a crown of lamb): she thought it wouldn't do his masculinity any good. Once she had insisted on sewing up the stuffed shoulders of lamb, saying she didn't want a 'seamstress' for a husband (which had nearly caused a row). But Ronald had put his foot down at this, and said that no part of *his* trade could make him *less* of a man!

Before finishing the window he started to arrange what Doreen called the 'washing line', which meant all the animal and bird bodies which he strung up outside his shop. First he hung the rabbits and hares. He put paper bags over their heads because he didn't like 'all that dripping blood messing up the pavement'. He made two holes in each bag to let the ears out – it amused him in a way. He also had a sense of humour, as well as a feeling for animals. While tying the bags round the necks, he felt something brushing his leg and bent down to feel what it was. It was Gladys their cat (who in fact was male but Cheryl, their daughter, ignored Gladys's gender and refused to rename him). As he passed his hand over Gladys – his trained butcher's hand which he likened to a surgeon's – he felt how similar Gladys's legs and fur were to the rabbits', and he took his hand away. At that same moment he remembered last night in bed, and the gale last night and the sort of nightmare he had had. Doreen had told him to 'Turn over and be a good lamb' (it had been a family joke once, but he hadn't laughed last night). Around the bedroom (which was above his shop) the wind had swirled, making his breathing taut so that in the long encasement of the bed he had felt his dark red blood being stirred, whipped up by the wind outside, and a dream inside, which had been stronger, fiercer than himself.

Above him, he heard the sound of shaking; he jumped, looked up and saw that it was Cheryl shaking the day-before out with a yellow duster. Cheryl was their only child and Cheryl was spoilt and had a perm in her ginger hair which had been there since she was nine when she had demanded it. He waved to her, a small wave, while Cheryl wondered why her father looked a little odd. She wished that he was a more 'presentable' man, a bigger man: but everyone said that he made up for his smallness by his neatness, especially in the finer aspects of his trade. And, she reminded herself, it wasn't for nothing that he was a member (honorary she thought it was) of the Tripe Dressers Associ-ation of Great Britain *and* Northern Ireland. Below her, her father squeezed his chamois leather cloth until his knuckles glinted. He told himself to stop 'dilly-dallying' and get on with the day's work. After all, it *was* his favourite (and most profitable) day of the year!

He went inside and washed his hands: over and over again he washed them during the day. Then he opened the door of the chiller (his freezer room). Once when he'd been working in the chiller, he'd developed backache, and after that Doreen had called it the 'spine chiller'. How they had laughed at that. He removed two suckling pigs which were suspended from hooks. They still had their eyelashes on and, 'dressed' in their smooth little pink skins which always seemed a size too big for them, it looked as though they were wearing Baby-gro clothes. He tucked one under each arm and carried them to his window, where he laid them in the centre. He remembered how, in the early years of his marriage, Doreen and he used to play 'little sausages' with each others' fingers. That was the time when Doreen, watch-ing him serving, used to think longingly of how she had been made love to by those hands which were plump and pink, but passionate. Doreen was now a proficient sausage-maker herself; he couldn't fault her. He put each pig's front left trotter over its right, as if they were relaxing in front of a fire – that would make Doreen and Cheryl laugh. But for some reason it didn't make him laugh, now.

Although the suckling pigs were his 'pièce de résistance' (he'd accumulated quite a bit of French from the different cuts of meat, like entrecôte and fillet), he preferred to keep the whole carcasses and large cuts of meat in the chiller for his best customers who bought his 'Combi Paks'. The lamb 'Pak' included a shoulder, best end of neck, leg, chump and loin chops. He also did a 'Pork Selection Pak' and a 'Miscellaneous Offal Assortment'. His best customers were the Grubbs, who probably had the biggest freezer in the district. Sometimes he wondered (a little uncharitably he knew) how the Grubbs, who must have spent most of their hours munching through the vast quantities of meat, ever had time to come and buy it.

The butcher went outside again to survey his work, saying, 'Happy Christmas' (beneath the brown autumn hedge of his moustache) to the people who passed in the street. Usually he admired his display, which was now three-quarters finished – almost like a jewellery shop window, he'd arranged it so meticulously. With the addition of Doreen's 'paarzley', and all the red and white, it was very 'Christmasy' and festive. But somehow he didn't like the arrangement: there was too much red – red everywhere . . . except for the salt beef, which was a dismal colour and shape and looked ill, as though suffering from anaemia, which it probably was after all that soaking in brine. It offended the artist in him. But he had to provide it.

He stopped looking at his window, and turned round to watch a train pass, a few fields away from his shop. The train smoke covered the black and white cows who galloped over the fields, their straight backs carrying the mounds of smoke. Over and over again they did it – it was a half-hour service – but still they were surprised. Showed how *unintelligent* they were, he thought, almost annoyed.

For quite some time the butcher, who had a small chest, stared into his shop, breathing slowly and shallowly while half remembering last night's dream. His fists were clenched; he began to almost hate his window, and the meat inside it. But it was past opening time and he knew he would have to go inside soon. But he didn't want to go in, or hold his £8.75 chopper which had always been his pride and joy. Every night, after polishing it, he hung it, by the hole in the end of its blade, at the side of his table.

He looked at the greengrocer's shop next door. There were mounds of mushrooms, which seemed to be under a spell, tomatoes which glowed, purple irises whose petals were as smooth as lips, and daffodils which were still filled with pollen even though they'd come all the way by jolting train from Bradford Greenhouses and Sons; the sons grew the smaller plants.

'Dad?' It was Cheryl, with their two dogs, Phyllis and Cyril. 'Phyllis looks a bit pale today,' she said. The butcher did a bit of greyhound racing at the weekends and Cyril was to be in the New Year Stakes.

'Well give them a good run, then,' the butcher replied, trying to buck himself up as he watched Cheryl (the apple of his eye) being towed along by the greyhounds who swallowed tablespoonfuls of air into their hollow-looking stomachs.

'Ron, I've done the turks!' Doreen called out, clutching a naked turkey which was almost half her size. When the turkeys were strung up they resembled old-fashioned flesh-coloured corsets hanging on a washing line. The butcher made a space between the turkeys and the furred animals, the combination of fur and feathers making him feel uneasy.

Then he thought he felt a drop of rain and smoothed his hand over his hair; he had what looked like a layer of brilliantine poured over his head in which was carefully embedded a few strands of hair. So he moved beneath the shelter of the awning. But then he felt another drop. When he touched his head, he saw it wasn't rain, but blood.

'Those *bloody* paper bags round the rabbits' heads are leaking, Doreen!' he said with sudden ferocity.

'OK, OK – keep your fur on. I always said those bags was stupid, everyone knows what's inside of them,' Doreen answered, surprised at his anger, before adding (seeing it was the season of goodwill), 'Besides, Ronald, the kiddies like looking at the rabbits' faces. I'll take the bags off of them in a minute,' she said soothingly.

'No! . . . Oh . . .' She didn't hear the end of his sentence because he had gone into his shop, forcing himself into it.

Ronald, Doreen concluded, was obviously overtired be-cause generally hardly a cross word passed between them. In fact Ronald didn't speak much at all, which Doreen thought was manly (like John Wayne in his more silent films); anyway, there were few pauses in her conversation for Ronald to fill. As well as being even-tempered, he was also reliable and dependable; he always sharpened the carv-ing knife with the same number of strokes each Sunday when carving their joint, *and* people used to ask his advice on all sorts of things: how to get pork crackling to really crackle – and even political things like the effect of inflation on the meat trade. His knowledge was vast and she loved him. And she really loved eating meat; it was a bond between them. If she wanted, she could eat meat three times a day, *and* have a few private ham sandwich 'fillers'. They also both enjoyed an occasional drink, though alcohol seemed to gallop to Doreen's head. Once, after a sherry trifle, she had had to be carried to bed.

At the back of his shop the butcher worked, his brown

skilled eyes close to the meat which he dismantled and chopped, with a heavy hand, sharpening and re-sharpening his knife as he prepared one Christmas order after another. The more he worked the colder his red hands became, although it wasn't cold in his shop. On the other side of his window some village children peered in at him. He didn't look back. He seemed, he noticed, to be making a bit of a mess, which was unusual for him. Through the ventilator, he heard the birds' short bursts of winter song, chopping the day up into pieces. His blue-and-white-striped apron (which had been spotless a short time ago) had blood on it; it was on his hands, too – everywhere; the thick smell of it made him feel sick.

He suddenly felt tired and cramped and stood up, bumping his head against a headless carcass which made it swing backwards and forwards, hitting the other carcasses so that they all began to swing. With one hand he steadied himself on an icy marble-topped table, and with the other he reached up to try and stop the dead animals swinging: it was becoming too much. But he couldn't reach because his arm seemed to have no energy in it and because he was a small man (though, as people said, he made up for his smallness by his neatness). But he wasn't neat now. He was hot, except for his frozen hands, and untidy, and he needed a breath of fresh air.

So he went into the chiller. In the semi-darkness he couldn't see properly, though he knew he was surrounded on three sides by meat. He felt something touching, tickling his head; he raised his hand and found it was a frozen chicken's foot combing through his hair. There were hanging carcasses in here, too, maroon and blue – frozen and stiff as sculpture. He began to shiver, although his right hand seemed suddenly hot, and energetic, and in it he felt his chopper hanging vertically against his apron, the stripes of which whipped round him horizontally. With one stroke he raised his chopper in the darkness . . . but his arm fell heavily to his side. Quickly he left the chiller.

Outside his shop the butcher saw his wife. She had come out of the kitchen when she had heard the noise in the chiller. Her face was sweating and her hands were wet as she'd just finished cooking. She cooked a lot so she was always partly covered in condensation. But no matter what she cooked she always smelt of bacon and eggs – even in the evening; he used to find this 'perfume' strangely seductive, but he didn't now: it made him feel sick again. Doreen smiled at him, a strained and painful smile because her mouth was filled with bread she'd been nibbling. She stood looking at her husband anxiously while holding Gladys.

The butcher left his shop and went into his house. He couldn't stay in his shop any longer; he couldn't be alone with the meat, but he couldn't tell Doreen this. Doreen told him to sit in the lounge and rest for a bit while she looked after the shop and, later, made him something to eat.

He sat down in one of their many leather-covered chairs. There were so many chairs (bought wholesale) in the lounge that they looked more like a herd of cattle, and they were so slippery that anyone sitting on them almost needed stirrups to prevent themselves sliding off.

Doreen decided to make Ronald something 'a little special', as he had said, she thought – although she could hardly hear him because he mumbled – that the meat was worrying him. She didn't know what he meant, so she cooked a whole kipper, adding half a slice of lemon to imitate an eye. He said he didn't want the eye. So she told him to 'Leave it there, love, it won't hurt you.'

As the butcher sat in his front room, fog started to descend again. Its head and shoulders were creeping through the large spaces in the scaffolding opposite his window. In the street he saw dim figures leading dogs on leads as they moved beneath the empty trees which had been clipped by winter.

The shining polished window of the darkened lounge reflected like a lake. And a hyacinth, still tightly in bud, on the table, seemed to be floating in a pool of darkness. At the back of the room, the bottom of the lake, a lamp bulb hung suspended from the ceiling like a weed, beneath which Cheryl moved, softly flitting with a yellow duster, while trying not to disturb her father whom she knew did not feel well. He looked so white in the dark room. Even his hands were white. As she moved around she looked more like a swimmer than someone walking.

Cheryl then left the room. As she did so, the butcher, sitting fathoms away from the window, suddenly placed his hand on his dog Cyril's tall warm back, as from the chiller he heard sounds of bumping, and of hooves scrambling. Out of it had clambered an animal: its head was a cow's, its forequarters pig and its hindquarters lamb. Slowly it moved towards him. Its eyes were kind, and blue, and they looked at the butcher. And the butcher, sealed to his chair, looked back.

The Trials

Cynthia Gunn awoke abruptly. She raised her head and listened . . . while within her a disturbing dream sank and became blurred . . . and deep countryside silence filled her bedroom. Her pink and white cheeks were imprinted with striped patterns from the candlewick bedspread which she always forgot to remove, because she liked the companionship of its weight. But the innocent colouring of her complexion (as well as the innocence of her expression) didn't blend with the first hints of greyness in her hair, which was rather coarse and crinkly, more akin to upholstery stuffing bursting from a chair than hair growing from a head − at least that was its usual appearance, until yesterday, when she had had it permed, especially for tomorrow.

'Move over, chaps. Leave some room for mother,' she addressed the dog and two cats who shared her bed. Violet, an elderly Pekinese who snored, settled herself into the small of Cynthia's large back, while Digby, a Siamese cat, lay across her legs, clamping them down. Cynthia, gazing round at all the fur which surrounded her, noticed how the animals appeared to grow in size and weight during the night, almost metamorphosing into different creatures. She lay down, stretched to her full six feet two inches (when her cream-coloured feet stuck out of the end of the bed) and endeavoured to rebury herself in the safety of sleep. But the sunken dream rose again: in it she was being chased by a dog; she was being hypnotized by it. She pressed her face into the pillow, squashing the dream. Obviously, she counselled herself, she was just nervous about tomorrow, even though it was her favourite day of the year.

At that moment, she felt the vibration of sheep's hooves running across the field outside her bungalow. The stampeding feet were followed by a low growl. She sat up, looking, with her tightly permed hair and buff viyella nightgown, not unlike a startled sheep herself.

'What stupid creatures sheep are. It's only Girly in her kennel.' Girly was the collie she had saved up for and finally bought, fully-trained, for sheep-dog trialling. Tomorrow they were going to compete in the County Championship which last year, to her amazement, she had won. The triumph of her success had lasted all through the year.

Next door, Jones, her parrot, whistled a few bars of *Strangers in the Night*. She tapped on the wall.

'It's still the middle of the night, laddie,' she informed him kindly. Jones became silent.

At six a.m. the sharp morning light squeezed itself between her closed eyelids. Digby and Humphrey, who watched over her like male nurses, tiptoed over the hills and valleys of her body, kneading her with their thumb-tip-sized paws. Through the narrow slit in her window came the sound of cat calls – gurgling, minor-keyed noises which were strong, almost scented, and disturbing. As though blindfold, her arm delved under the dusty bed for one of her size nine shoes, which she flung against the wall.

'Shut up, Please!' Neutered Digby and Humphrey (his uncle) sat up and looked at Cynthia, who saw herself reflected twice in the intense blue of Digby's unblinking oriental eyes. She put her hand out to stroke him, but something about his expression made her withdraw.

It was time to get up. Cynthia washed bits of herself in a

small hand-basin which was just large enough for her hands and a guest-size piece of soap. She cleaned her teeth; she had a lot of teeth and so had her younger brother Ginger. That so many teeth should have been distributed between only two people seemed over-generous. Now, she didn't see Ginger, or many other people. People were so difficult to get on with ... except of course for her sheep-dog-trialling friends. Animals were easier, she thought. And plants. Cynthia Gunn worked in a market-garden.

She went to her wardrobe, part of which was occupied by cricket bats left over from her Leeds University days when she'd attempted to get a degree in chemistry. Several bats clattered to the floor, startling Cynthia who always took time to wake up properly. Sleep (the only place where she felt completely safe) acted upon her like a drug, pulling her down into its depths from which, in the morning, she had to clamber painfully out into the even more painful reality of the day. She put on a garment which was made of wool from her own small flock of Jacob sheep. Despite the smallness of the flock, the garment was very long, so it was difficult to tell whether it was a jumper which had slunk downwards or a dress which had shrunk upwards. Like most of the clothes she wore, it smelled very faintly of biscuits – Digestive. She then put on a pair of trousers which she had converted from a party skirt her mother had helped her to make before she had left home to go to university.

'You probably won't need it for parties, dear,' Mrs Gunn had said, finding it difficult to imagine her daughter being invited to parties. 'Of course I will,' Cynthia had replied. But she had quickly apologized, while her mother, crouching far below her, had struggled with the two-and-three-quarter yards of sale material, printed with large leaves from different deciduous trees. Mrs Gunn, who had felt her colossal daughter towering above her (more like a building than a daughter), could have hit her, her height made her so angry. Nothing fitted! And she had tugged at an elm leaf. 'What a lump you are,' she had said, from the side of her mouth which wasn't occupied by pins. But the sentence had still been audible. Cynthia, perhaps accustomed to Mrs Gunn's bark being worse, apparently, than her bite, had looked down into her mother's steel-grey hair and thought how strong she was.

Cynthia combed her hair; at least she tried to, but the comb couldn't cope with the dense undergrowth of tightly permed curls which looked and felt as though they'd been screwed into her head, giving her a flushed, ferocious expression. She glanced shyly in the mirror: the overgrown grey-haired schoolgirl who looked back didn't appear to own or be comfortable inside her body.

'You look rather like a lady farmer,' she chortled to herself; but it was almost as if she regretted laughing, the way her laughter creaked out.

'Come on, boys. And you, Violet dear. It's breakfast time and Girly and I must soon be off.' Violet, who was overweight, prepared herself for the drop from the bed to the floor, the fear of the eighteen-inch precipice almost overwhelming her desire for food. Cynthia removed an assortment of fur from the sheets, oblivious to what the Cheltenham branch of the Sunlight laundry might think when her mixed-fur sheets arrived to be washed.

From the front room came the sound of barking. Cynthia looked round, a mixture of fear and anger in her eyes: surely Girly hadn't escaped from her kennel? She went into the front room whose only occupant was Jones. Jones was an experienced mimic. Feeling both relieved and ridiculous, she raised the cover from his cage.

''ello, 'ello!' Jones said in a provocative old man's voice (inherited from his previous owner), while eyeing Cynthia with his grey, knowing eyes.

''ello, my darlin',' she mimicked affectionately, her wide knees cracking like firewood as she bent to look at him.

She then prepared the boys' breakfast. They always had raw meat for a treat on Saturdays. While she cut it up they moved to and fro between her legs, weaving an invisible web in which her two solid feet were implanted.

'Oh you are a couple!' she said. The cats bit voluptuously into the bright red meat, their eyes closed, their tails flat on the ground. Violet, who suffered from chestiness, watched, breathing heavily, her *retroussé* nose damp and her Bette Davis eyes watery and emotional. Then, miraculously defying gravity, she jumped onto Cynthia's lap and ate her Good Boy Choc Drops. Cynthia kissed Violet's moustached face, smelling her milk-chocolate breath. In response, Violet hiccuped.

'Pardon!' Cynthia Gunn liked good manners. Violet gazed back, her expression replete and forlorn.

Cynthia peeled Jones's grapes and ate the skins; they were good roughage, she'd informed him, but the fruitarian gourmet ignored the information and just perched upside down.

From the garden, small whimpering noises came from Girly's kennel.

'Wait! Your turn will come,' Cynthia called out. After Digby and Humphrey had washed each other, they watched Jones, from a distance – fur and feathers separated. She then prepared herself some sandwiches, on her lap, using sardines, which she boned. With one large hand she pressed the bread down and with the other she absent-mindedly swung the sardines' back-bones between her fingers. She enjoyed these community meals with the animals. They made *her* feel motherly, and her bungalow feel homely – or how she imagined a home would feel.

'Well, that's that, fellows. Now it's Girly's turn.' Cynthia fetched a bowl of dog biscuits. She ate one; she'd always

liked them and wondered why people didn't serve them
with drinks. 'DARLING' was dribbled in blue glaze on
the dog bowl, because 'Darling' was what she had originally
called Girly. Cynthia had always longed to call someone,
anyone, 'Darling'. And no one, especially her parents who
were against displays of extravagant emotion, had called her
this. The closest she had got was being called 'Luv' in Leeds.
'Darling' had been rejected by the Sheep Dog Trial Auth-
orities. 'What is the dog, anyway?' they had asked her on
the telephone, 'A dog or a bitch?' 'It's a girly dog,' she had
replied, strenuously avoiding the word bitch. What she had
thought might be laughter had filled the earpiece of her
telephone, so she had joined in, and called the dog Girly.

Cynthia went into the garden. Peering through the gap
between the door and the floor of the kennel was Girly's
long shining nose, and above it her watchful eyes. One was
blue and one was brown, which was why Cynthia had
bought her. At times, though, as she looked at each eye
individually, this gave her a curiously uncomfortable feeling, especially when Girly was in her kennel, its dark
creosoted walls resembling a hood on a bird of prey. As
soon as Girly heard Cynthia, she leapt up inside the kennel
which sounded as if it would burst apart with her restrained
energy and enthusiasm.

'Down girl!' commanded Cynthia, in the tone she had
been taught by Girly's original owner. Girly sank obediently
to the ground. Cynthia rewarded her submission with dog
biscuits, while stroking her smooth warm head judiciously.
She felt in charge – as her mother must have felt when
instilling discipline into her children, rewarding only when
rewards were due. She had learnt a lot from her mother, she
thought – even though the Gunns had never allowed animals
into their house, considering them dirty and risky. Marvellous old mother, thought Cynthia, her thoughts, tenderized

by time and the need to love, circumnavigating the rock-like Mrs Gunn.

It was time to leave for the trials. In case some of the lads came back with her after the show (as they had last year) she did a little tidying (as she had not done last year). She blew the surface dust from some of the more prominent objects and adjusted her birth certificate on the mantelpiece. Since its edges had started to disintegrate, she had put it into a frame, the sight of it apparently confirming, to her, that she had in fact been born.

She closed the door of Jones's cage, through the bars of which he looked at her, making her feel she was being observed by a solicitor. She popped Violet into a sleeveless reversible cardigan which had a pocket. For what? Then she picked up Humphrey and stroked him, wiping the purr from his body as she stroked – until she saw Digby watching. Eight eyes from four corners of the room observed her, the animals' presence suddenly making the room feel smaller and fuller, and Cynthia feel uneasy.

'Cheerio, chaps, see you later,' she called out brightly, as half-guiltily she locked the front door. I wish, she said to herself, I could leave a note for the animals to say I've gone to the trials but *will* be back later.

She opened the door of her van, which had a metal grid to separate her from the animal passenger, similar to that in a police van.

'Car!' she commanded and Girly, her tail between her legs, leapt like a guilty prisoner from her kennel to the car.

The drive to the trial field reminded Cynthia of her time at university, 'being broadened out at a considerable cost to the nation', as the Gunns senior had frequently reminded her. (The guilt of her failure to pass her second-year examinations still made her feel crumpled inside, so she tried to avoid remembering it.) Although, during this time, she had longed to be visited or go home, she had seen little of her parents; they said it was for the sake of her independence, and because her visits disorganized things. However, they had arranged for her to go out walking with her friends and contemporaries the Aitchisons, and occasionally Mrs Gunn had sent her a food parcel which she had enjoyed unwrapping, undoing all the knots with her big athletic fingers, while imagining her mother taking part in a knot-contest with her. The parcel generally contained what Cynthia called a 'fudge cake', the recipe for which required a large quantity of elderly biscuits and not a lot of skill in the culinary arts.

She eyed Girly through the rear mirror and smiled proudly. Girly yawned, her white teeth gleaming behind the metal bars. They were nearly there. Cynthia felt pangs of stage fright. She might not have been successful in getting a degree, but surely her parents would have been proud about her winning the trial cup. So, no doubt, would the Aitchisons. They were between sixty and seventy years old – even then – and on every third Sunday of the month they had collected her in their car. She had to rush to finish her breakfast before they arrived. They always walked in a circle over the moors (Mr Aitchison had a compass), during which time Cynthia had battled with her indigestion. But it had never been chronic, and she had felt privileged, even though Mrs Aitchison, on the rare occasions when she spoke, called her husband Mr Aitchison in front of her. But Cynthia had counteracted this by using their Christian names (Maud and Arnold) privately to herself. After the walk they returned to the Aitchisons' home where they all had a bath – Cynthia last. But she hadn't minded about the tepid water – because it was in their home. After the baths, they ate a light salad supper on their laps and watched the television instead of talking.

Cynthia turned off the road and bounced across the trial

field. She let out Girly who rushed round and round – a gale on a lead. The triallers and dogs greeted each other, laughing and barking. She peered round for her friend Percy. It was Percy who had told her, when she had asked how long it took to train a dog, 'A year to train each leg and if it's a bad dog another year for the tail.' He hadn't explained that some people can never train a dog: to her shame Cynthia was one of them. In the same way that she didn't know why she couldn't get on with people, she also knew that she was not too good with animals. Part of her feared them, which was why (despite trying) she had had to buy a trained dog, thinking that the purchase was her best route into local life. Now, though, she had almost forgotten the particularities of the purchase, and hoped that the other triallers had, too. They had not.

''ello, my old gel,' said Percy, and they felled blows on each other's backs, despite the difference in height.

'How's Perce?' She tried, not very successfully, to imitate the local dialect. Percy was a dapper man who wore a speckled hat, yellow leather shoes and a thick faded gold wedding-ring which had embedded itself in his finger.

''ows the winner, then?' Claud, another trialler, asked Cynthia, who, never quite certain if people were joking or not, always heralded the mere signal of a joke with hoots of merriment – for safety's sake.

As everyone waited expectantly for the arrival of the judge, the tea-urn became as dry as the triallers' throats, and was refilled over and over again. Inside a canvas-covered trailer, five amber-eyed sheep huddled, shivering in the summer sun, in their 100% virgin wool coats. Through the canvas cover they heard the sound of dogs' barks tearing at the warm silky air. The sheep were pulled reluctantly from the van and led to a pen, where they waited like schoolgirl hostages.

Finally, the judge arrived. He wore a flat green hat (as

green as the field) which made him appear to be sandwiched
between hat and field. The trials began. Percy was the first
competitor.

'Thurr goes ol' tin whistle,' Claud said playfully, a hot-
dog sausage disappearing into the tunnel of his mouth.

Eventually it was Cynthia Gunn's turn. She released
Girly from her lead and, summoning her courage, strode,
slightly stooping, to the post where she stuck her shepherd's
crook into the ground. It stood, silhouetted in the shape of a
giant question mark. She whistled. Girly (and surprisingly
no other dog) joined her at the post. The sheep were
released from their pen. She whistled again and Girly rushed
off, low over the ground, like a fox, her fur brushing the
short grass as she ran towards the sheep. Keeping a wide
cunning distance between herself and the flock, she herded
them hypnotically: a cat stalking mice. The sheep trotted
forwards sedately and then stopped. Girly stopped, her
cocked ears cupping every sound. She crouched, her head
parallel with the ground, her mouth open, her pink, lolling
tongue dripping saliva, while her mesmeric eyes drove the
sheep closer and closer together until they became one ten-
legged animal, pinned together by fear. Across the wide
field Girly and Cynthia communicated with each other in
the language she had inherited, and thought she had
mastered. At the slightest whistle, the dog stopped or started,
the power contained within her body released or restrained
by an invisible cord. Cynthia knew that it was only her
commands which held in check the instinct of the hungry,
murderous dog. It was the epitome of discipline, an extension of the code which her parents had taught her and
from which she hoped she would never deviate.

She was doing well. She felt the spectators' admiration
behind her, warm and supporting – like a vast family. Inside
closed cars, envious dogs of other breeds sat upright in the
drivers' seats, resembling chauffeurs. The sheep were now

approaching the pen. Cynthia felt exhilarated, and moved slowly towards the pen gate, ready to close it. But then, suddenly, the sheep scattered and Girly was racing towards the other side of the field, the springy turf beneath her paws.

'Girl!' Cynthia's voice boomed across the field. What was going to be applause turned into muttering.

'If a dog don't feel loike it on the day there's nothin' you can do about it,' Percy told a spectator. Sweat trickled down Cynthia Gunn's wide white forehead while she supported herself on her shepherd's crook. She called and whistled, the long and short whistles like some strange bird; the tenor-voiced sheep baaed tremulously. Supposing, she thought in a hot flush of fear, that Girly's gone off and attacked a sheep in another field?

Behind the spectators' rope, Claud explained to two visitors about the fine dividing line between a dog attacking or guiding sheep.

'It's loike this. If a dog suddenly becomes a killer, no matter 'ow good 'e is, 'e 'as to be put down, as once 'e 'as a taste furr sheep, furr blood, there's no way of changin' 'im. And they become so cunnin', too. They'll saunter off, lookin' innocent enough – loike you or me goin' to the pub – go to another farmer's field, catch a sheep and then wash thoroughly before comin' 'ome.'

A few minutes later, over the brow of the hill Girly's dark body crept, dark as a storm cloud. Slowly she walked towards her mistress.

The trialling came to an end. The cup was presented to Percy's nephew.

'Never moind,' consoled Claud, 'you'll save on the silver polish!' Cynthia tried to smile.

'See you at home then, lads, as usual, for some grub,' she asked rather than stated, in her least successful attempt at the local dialect. And off she drove, Girly hot and damp in the back. Cynthia Gunn did not look at her in the driving mirror.

When she arrived home she returned Girly to her kennel. Then she opened the front door and nearly fell over the bundle of animals who rushed to greet her, tails wagging and waving.

Cynthia prepared a meal for the lads; she liked to give them something manly. This consisted of a khaki-coloured stew from which chicken thighs, and what appeared to be ankles and knees, protruded. (Claud had once told Percy that 'our Cynth' was the only cook he knew who bought breastless chickens with three legs.) She worked quickly, chopping and cutting – and cutting out the possibility, which lurked in her mind, that they might not come, because she had failed. The stew was to be followed by a very bright, very stiff jelly which, when entered by the eater's spoon, was apt to catapult it forwards, making sucking noises. Certain that she would be the winner of the cup, she had remembered (as she had not done last time) to buy the lads some beer which she considerately, but ill-advisedly, opened in readiness for their arrival.

She then hurriedly prepared herself, dabbing on scent from a bottle which her great aunt had left unopened before she had passed over. Then (many years ago), Cynthia hadn't minded about death and had dabbed the scent on freely. Now, it was nervousness which made her so generous with it.

There was a knock at the door. Percy and Claud entered.

''ello me old lass. Good smell's comin' from the kitchen, then!' said Percy.

'And from our Cynth, too!' Claud added, in his best party manner. Cynthia tried, unsuccessfully, to suppress a rising blush. Claud went over to the birdcage. ''ello, Smith,' he said to Jones, who opened his ancient lid a millimetre or two, eyeing him through the slit before closing it.

'He's called Jones,' Cynthia reminded him.

'You're a stickler furr formalities, Cynth.' And they all laughed, drinking their flat beer while rocking to and fro on their toes.

She brought in the stew. When they had finished it looked, with the plates piled high with bones, as though a dog's banquet had taken place. For a long time they discussed the trials; Cynthia felt ashamed and small. Not wanting to spoil the evening, she tried to combat these feelings by bringing in the cheerful jelly. But the noises it made didn't assist the party.

'Well, where's the culprit, then?' Claud asked.

'Girly's in her kennel.'

'Why not bring 'er in 'ere, for a treat?'

'It's not a treat she needs, and I never bring her inside; she's a working dog.'

'Oh go on. Won't 'urt furr once, will it Perce?'

'Dou-tit,' Percy said doubtfully. Not wanting to be a spoil-sport, she fetched Girly. Girly, astonished by this reversal in her routine, leapt up and licked everyone frantically, until Cynthia said, 'Down!' Girly slunk beneath the table and lay there, rug-like. Above her head they continued to discuss trialling.

'Course your Girly's got a strong eye to stare out the sheep. There's dogs with very strong eyes 'ho get so invalved that the trialler loses touch with them. And there's dogs with weak eyes and butterfly minds, who the cunnin' old ewes can run circles round.' Cynthia gradually revived and felt proud, as though she'd been the provider of Girly's strong eye. At the same moment she felt something almost touching her. She looked down and saw Girly's head stretched out flat on her paws: the strong beams from the dog's eyes rose upwards, holding her eyes. Cynthia shifted her chair, trying to concentrate on what the men were saying. But she couldn't. No matter where she looked her gaze was dragged down to Girly's, as though she were being pulled inside the animal eyes. She felt hot; and then, strangely for a warm evening, a coldness started to spread through her. She put her hands into the sleeves of her jumper, warming and holding herself. Girly continued to gaze up, while Digby, Humphrey, Violet and Jones looked on silently. Cynthia stood up, feeling she had to do something, anything to move away from Girly's stare. She wasn't frightened, she told herself; she just wasn't accustomed to having Girly in the house and being confronted by her at such close quarters. She was still in command. But her fear continued to leak from her, while in the back of her mind the memory of last night's dream began to surface again.

'Can I 'elp?' Percy offered.

'I . . . I was going to give the dog some biscuits.' She felt huge, awkward and naked in the room, in comparison with the seated men and flattened dog.

'I'll get 'em.' Percy held a handful of biscuits under the table. Girly didn't move. 'I think she's asleep. Probably whacked out.' Cynthia moved to another chair. The black and white furred shape in the dim light under the table shifted to face her. Cynthia held her head upright, forcing herself not to look down, while her stomach contracted into a small, hard lump. *Why* can't she look elsewhere, at someone else? she thought in panic and anger. She felt sick, got up and went to the kitchen, closing the door. She leant against it, her long legs feeling wobbly. But I must go back, she thought, or what will they think? What would mother think? Her panic doubled. She tried to breathe deeply. I'll ask them to put Girly back in her kennel — say I'm just feeling a little poorly. Just as she was about to open the door she heard scratching noises on the other side of it. Violet's elderly nails were too brittle to make such sharp, persistent sounds.

Cynthia dashed across the kitchen, opened the back door and went out into the night. An unseen owl hooted from the dark branches of a tree. She looked round in alarm. There was nowhere to go. Then she heard the men's voices calling.

'Cynth? Where are you?' The voices grew louder. 'Miss Gunn? You a'right?' They must have opened the front door: Girly would soon be out. Cynthia ran to the sheep-shed and closed the door. Inside, surrounded and blindfolded by the darkness (and with the dog outside), she felt frightened and then angry, hating the fear. She realized that it wasn't a new sensation; her parents had sometimes made her feel like this – and so had most people. Her anger grew until she felt like smashing the shed; but she was immobilized by the blackness. Never, she swore, did she want to feel like this again. She would get rid of Girly, and stop the ridiculous trialling of which she had never been a part. It was hateful, this distortion of a dog's instincts, and abuse of the sheep's fear.

Outside, the men's voices spoke in the dark, punctuated by sniffing sounds from Girly which grew closer.

'Girly!' Cynthia's voice, imitated by Jones, shouted in the house.

'She's in the 'ouse, then!' the men's voices exclaimed in unison.

'*No I'm not*, I'm in here, in the sheep-shed. Take Girly away. *Please*. I'm frightened of her – she needs another home – and I don't want to do any more trialling.' She opened the door an inch. A few tufts of wool were attached to her permed hair. The men looked at her and she looked back at them. They felt it was the first time they had really seen her: suddenly they could feel her presence. And her frightened, yet determined, voice had more conviction in it now than it had ever had on the field.

Mrs F. Pearson-Bent

Up and down the long dark passage of her London basement flat Mrs F. Pearson-Bent walked, stepping like a moorhen in her good narrow shoes. On either side of her the empty rooms stood, a silent guard of honour, the doorknobs shining as brightly as medals, twisting her image in brass around their handles. For a second she stopped, tightened a silver earring and, in case she had an accident and was brought home, she went into the bathroom and unwrapped the soap (which had an Eastern scent) which she would wrap up again when she came home. She was almost ready to go out.

Mrs Pearson-Bent had been seventy-nine for some years now (said her friends who were eighty-three, five and nine, over Fuller's cake, in pastel shades, and tea from a silver tea-pot). She had been married, 'To a fine man – your Uncle Frank,' she always reminded her great nephew. She would use her husband's initial for as long as she lived. Those were his books under the silent glass case: Scott bound in green and gold, from volume one to volume fourteen. That was the advantage of Scott: he always looked nice and could be relied upon to occupy the first shelf.

After adjusting the lace curtain of her modesty vest, she was ready to go out. Then she remembered her nephew, who was sitting on the chair, which had a straight back, in the hall. Had he been sitting there since two o'clock? He opened the door for her and out they went.

Twice a year, on a Sunday, she invited this small boy to stay.

'Hold my hand while we cross the road.' There was no traffic and the nephew held her hand as loosely as possible and only for the crossing. 'It's strange to see you growing up,' she said.

'And it's strange to see you growing – too,' he answered in his politest voice, while watching his great-aunt being blown about the pavement. Was she being blown by a wind he didn't feel? Or was she *very* old?

Her feet, she thought, were stepping well in her good shoes; her body was upright; and she received letters nearly every day. But I have suddenly grown older and can't remember things: that coffee is bad for me, and that I have had coffee-fever, which was due to my maid, Mrs Dod, who boiled and boiled it.

That must be one of the Miss Darlings walking towards us. I shall offer her some wax flower-cuttings (I am probably one of the most generous people I know) when she comes to tea on Thursday. And she will say, 'How wonderful to have something fresh and green in the house.'

Miss Darling had her name written in sloping handwriting on all the Thursdays in Mrs Pearson-Bent's diary. She came to tea in faded green dresses which she also wore when weeding amongst the mint and thyme in her garden. Miss Darling asked Mrs Pearson-Bent if she could 'manage' this Thursday, and the old lady looked through the white pages of her diary and said she might 'with a little squeeze', fit her in before four. Miss Darling seemed delighted with the offer of the wax flower-cuttings, which would break in the breeze and melt when the sun came out. She would put them next to the porcelain sheep whose wool coat scratched when stroked but was accurate, in porcelain, to the last curl.

'Well, we must be going. I'm taking my nephew to the park and then we shall ride on a bus. I can remember, when

I was a girl in China, how we used to be taken for rides in a jig-saw . . .'

They had reached the house of one of Uncle Frank's acquaintances. He was an old gentleman who wore a suit which appeared to have been made out of brown bread (wholemeal). He had a large London garden, inside which was a weathercock, empty dovecot and a rocking horse, which were all painted white at the same time of year. Huge toys they were, spread about the lawn. The rocking horse was bolted down so it couldn't rock, even in the roughest weather, when the wind would butt and tug at it and the rain rotted its real horsehair mane.

After tea, they left the old gentleman, in his squeaking wicker chair, following the sun around his garden.

Into the park they walked. Soon, thought the great-nephew, he could sail his boat, watched over by his great-aunt, who creaked when she stooped to help him launch his boat, while gripping his arm with cast-iron fingers to prevent him drowning (death by misadventure) in Kensington Round Pond, which was only eighteen inches deep, after heavy rain. He watched the handmade sailing boats lean towards the water, wetting their sails which were pushed out by the breeze and their owners' longing for a bigger sea. Perhaps there's a whirlpool, he thought, and moved towards the water, or a subterranean gale (she held on to him tightly), which makes the sailing boat revolve all Sunday afternoon instead of sailing out to the middle of the pond to wait for the weekend breeze to send it racing across to the other side (faster than I can run) to shipwreck on the dangerous cement shore. With giant fingers he picked up his dripping boat and slackened the ropes – a piece of pyjama cord. It was getting a little dark. They walked towards the bus stop.

I mustn't run or my face will drain of all colour when I mount the stairs of the bus. What a height! Into a food shop window the nephew looked, where frogs, which were made from gherkins and other green things, beat vol-au-vent drums, and everything which did anything was made of food. Figures with puff pastry heads, almond eyes, marzipan hips and custard insides (by kind permission of Bird's) danced all night in the lighted window.

The bus stopped at the lights, beside another bus. There were privileges to be had from riding in the tops of buses; you could look right into this man's face, that woman's eyes, with only the glass to separate the gazes. Mrs Pearson-Bent looked into the face, the eyes of the man opposite. So close they sat that the slightest movement of the lips might have been a kiss ... until the man looked back. Did she know him, she wondered. Mr Silvery was an artist and wore light greens and an occasional dark pink in summer; the colours blended perfectly. In and out of perspective he went as he looked at his reflection superimposed on the old lady opposite – for whom, many years ago, he had done a little restoration work; but this he had forgotten. I am an artist, he acknowledged, and probably the most sensitive person on this bus. I shouldn't be here, on buses in London. I should be in Italy, in Palermo – which he pronounced with an almost perfect roll of the 'r'. He half closed his eyes and saw everything in tones and half-tones; raw sienna in the old lady's face, burnt umber (what words!) in the boy's eyes.

'After one more stop we must disembark and return home, because I don't want you to go to bed late.' The nephew hated his great-aunt's words and looked into a shop window which was being dressed for Monday. Flesh-tinted dummies, which had cardboard breasts and no movement in their perfect bodies, held hands which didn't feel and stood in gay abandon. 'Gay abandon!' shouted the head window-dresser, who wore socks all day until he went home and changed into slippers. 'Cover them up or dismantle them; one or the other! I won't have indecency in my windows!' he shouted to the under window-dressers. So they put stockings on the dummies' hollow legs and unrolled raffia lawns for them to stand on and look 'summery'.

The 'a' from Sainsbury's was missing, Mrs Pearson-Bent noticed, almost affronted. But everyone knew it was Sainsbury's. That, she supposed, was common sense – no, more than that, one of the secrets of being British. She sat up straight, feeling moved and patriotic, and decided to ride every Sunday on the top of a bus. It was time to disembark.

'Go carefully down the stairs, child.' The 'child' suspended himself on the stair rails and swung his feet in the air.

Mrs Pearson-Bent guided her nephew's arm past a pet-shop window, behind which a cat lay amongst the tall wool of a rug. For this was a reliable shop where the bird seed was delivered fortnightly and the poodles were sold already clipped.

When they arrived at the old lady's flat, darkness reached right down to the ground and rain dripped from the leafless trees.

'Can I have a night-light, please?' the nephew asked, hoping his mother would come early in the morning to collect him. His great-aunt gave him the remains of a night-light; its flame flickered backwards and forwards, trying to avoid the water in the saucer, before it went out with a sizz. He got into the bed, whose white sheets had turned black in the darkness . . . Perhaps someone had died in the bed. His toes touched a cold copper bottle. Then his great-aunt came into the room.

'Good night, child,' she said, kissing his forehead with her straight mouth and putting her cold soft hand on his head. Then she left. For a long time he waited to hear her getting into bed in the next room . . . Perhaps she had died and they would bury her: her body would moulder among the roots of violets and dandelions in the dark damp earth, and being dead would be like having one's eyes closed for ever and ever.

Mrs Pearson-Bent went into her bedroom. The window had been left open all day so that while she had been away the room had become filled with sounds and scents, impressions she hadn't heard or seen. It was like entering a party of silent people, guessing at what she hadn't heard. She combed her hair, in case anyone called. But no one came, so she remained neat all evening. She sat down and crossed-and-stitched a little further round a laurel leaf, using a darker green for the underside, while reminding herself that the correct, exact shade for laurel was number twenty-six in Craft Silks.

Later she undressed; folded her silk scarf down and across using the right creases; pushed shoe-trees into the dark tips of shoes, and rolled mothballs between her grey camisole. All this she did late at night with just her bedside lamp on, to economize, moving around in the small amount of faded light, between the pale shadows which lay like tired animals on the floor. Moving with quick footsteps, she tidied and tidied until everything was as tidy as it was before she had started. Then she got into bed and lay down, waiting for the next day to come rolling over the hills and into London, where it would drop through the window into her basement flat.

She was ready.

Good Friday

Mrs Smiley woke early in her slim bedroom. It was the first time she had ever woken up in London, her life (after her husband, Arthur, had been killed at the end of the war) having been spent in the country as housekeeper to Miss Hunter who, only recently, had decided to return to London.

Smiley (as she was called by Miss Hunter) stretched carefully on the two-foot-six-inch bed which had been allotted to her, beneath which a small orchestra of springs and coils twanged and snapped. Strong sunlight pressed against the thick curtains which kept the morning at bay outside the window until, unable to resist, she drew back the curtains with both hands – hands which looked as if they had been borrowed from an older woman. She returned to her bed, lay down – covered by the warm blanket of air – and smiled, the corners of her smile tucked into the folds of her cheeks. She listened. A milk-float hummed down the street, sounding like a contented cleaner, its bottles jangling. A taxi, shiny as a blackcurrant pastille, stopped outside a door, purring. Who had it delivered or collected at such an early hour? These were quite different from the country sounds of Dorset, the place of her birth.

Ever since Miss Hunter had mentioned that she might return to London, where she had spent her youth, Mrs Smiley had been looking forward to it. The daylight had now erased the ripple of fear she had felt during the night when, standing at her window, she had heard the screams of other windows being opened and closed – the black open windows breathing in the night air of Onslow Square. Later, in the depths of the night, she had woken again, sensing the city all around her, its breath held: a great animal waiting to pounce, or ... Waiting for what? For it all to start up again in the morning, she supposed. But these thoughts, she had consoled herself, were just dark nocturnal thoughts. It would be different in the morning.

She stretched to her full four-feet-eleven-inches, hardly able to wait until she could go shopping in the Super Market. Her cousin had told her all about Super Markets; she might buy her a late Easter egg. In the country, most of Miss Hunter's provisions had been delivered from the nearest town, the rest Mrs Smiley had bought from the one and only village shop, which was also the post office; and it would certainly be closed today, Good Friday: its owners would be at church.

Five more minutes passed. She could wait no longer, got out of bed (moving as quietly as she could so as not to disturb Miss Hunter), washed, and combed her short hair, which had the same sheen as some birds' feathers have, even though it was nearly white. Then she put on her small clothes, most of which she had ordered from a mail-order catalogue – children's section. It was less embarrassing that way. When she was on her own, she spent hours searching happily through the catalogue for the most grown-up look-ing of the children's fashions.

After squeezing Miss Hunter's orange juice, she laid out the rest of her breakfast. Then, holding the shopping list which she had been handed the previous evening, she opened the front door. Before stepping into the sunshine which filled the cavern-like spaces between the streets of houses, she made certain that the artificial belt on the back of her sage-green coat was in place. (It was this little touch of 'fashion' which had decided her on this particular model.) She turned round to see that the number of the house and the name of the street corresponded with those in her memory; they did, so there was no need to write them down. And off she set, walking quietly along the Easter streets in her winter boots.

It was a beautiful Good Friday, the breezes patient and warm as they lolled at the street corners. On her shoulders the air rested, warm, soft and light as Miss Hunter's cashmere cardigans. The thoughts in her head (now she was out of the house) felt gentle and happy. The sun was out. It lay stretched across a small public garden, gilding the vacant benches on which it lazed, convalescing after winter. But the park gate was locked. She was about to ask someone when it would be unlocked, but by the time she had opened her mouth, they had already passed. She closed her mouth, feeling the outside air inside it. Perhaps it was still too early in the day to speak to people in London. Although the park was closed, through its high diamond-shaped fencing escaped the thick velvety scent of wallflowers. It seemed strange to her that plants should be locked in.

Mrs Smiley decided that until she got to know a few London people, she would chat to passing dogs. And what better place to do that, she discovered, than outside the Super Market itself, where, to her surprise, she found a whole selection of waiting dogs.

Mrs Smiley looked at them; they looked back at her. There was a poodle who appeared to have been knitted out of bouclé wool. He was dressed in a red showerproof boiler suit (with a zip) which reached right down to his ankles. It made *her* clothes feel quite provincial. Despite the suit he shivered continually in the sun. Most country dogs, she remembered, still went round naked. Other dogs were busy peering between the opening and closing of the glass doors for a glimpse of their owners' feet. Then a basket on wheels appeared, inside which a peke, ensconced on a rug amidst rolls of lavatory paper, digestive biscuits and tonic water, peered out rather smugly at the other wheel-less dogs.

Just as Mrs Smiley was about to enter the shop, a young man in a wheelchair was parked outside with the dogs. His hands fluttered close to his body, like caged birds, and his head rolled skywards and then swung dizzily to face the pavement. Surely, she thought in astonishment, he's not just going to be left there? Even the dogs are tied up. Then slowly she realized that he would hardly be stolen. She pushed against the heavy glass doors, as though to escape from her thoughts into the shop. But the doors were too heavy for her, and one of them had what resembled a huge elastoplast across it. Had someone hungry tried to break it? Then a man held open the door for her with his signet-ringed hand. She thanked him with a little movement of her body which was almost a curtsy, smiled and entered the shop.

So *this* was a Super Market, she exclaimed to herself. Never had she seen so many people shopping in one place, or such a huge shop. She couldn't see to the end of it; it was just a horizon.

Observing what the other shoppers did, she selected a trolley, which reached up to her ribs, and wheeled it away, enjoying the feeling of it gliding over the marble floor. Between one of the food avenues she glided, in her winter boots, partnered by the trolley; she might almost have been dancing with Arthur again. Arthur had been a wonderful waltzer. She could hardly stop, until accidentally she collided lightly into the hips of a large woman who stopped suddenly in front of her.

'Excuse *me*!' said the woman in a voice which sounded as if it would excuse nothing.

'Oh I am sorry. I hope I didn't hurt you.'

'This isn't the M1 motorway, you know!' Then in a tone which was far from confidential, she said to her husband, 'If people can't drive their trolleys responsibly, they shouldn't be let loose with them!' The husband, who followed her, dog-like, as though on a short invisible lead, nodded wearily.

Carefully Mrs Smiley manoeuvred the bulky trolley into the main aisle where she could practise 'driving', and at the end of which, she discovered, a whole section of the shop was devoted to cakes and bread. Her soft brown eyes gazed entranced at marzipan Easter rabbits with edible whiskers, Easter-bonnet sponge-cakes with icing-sugar bows and hot cross buns (reduced in price).

High above, a huge clock swallowed a second, audibly. She looked up. It was nine o'clock already. She would have to hurry; so she started searching for the poultry department and Miss Hunter's skinned and boned chicken breast. But all she could see were rows of big-bosomed turkeys with bruised-looking goose-fleshed thighs. She tried to lift a bird, just to feel it, but it was as heavy and hard as cement.

'I thought people only ate turkeys at Christmas,' she said aloud. A man in a hurry looked blankly at her. Perhaps, she thought, they only speak at Christmas, too.

Then she saw the cream counter: double, single, clotted, whipping and long-life. She had always assumed that cream was cream. What did they do with the differences? And which one would Miss Hunter want? The choice was almost threatening.

Darjeeling tea was the next item on her list. She wheeled her trolley all round the outskirts of the food avenues, just in case the tea was at the end of a shelf. But it wasn't, so she would have to enter the aisles again.

'You don't want to leave your 'andbag in there in ye trolley.' An elderly woman had spoken to her.

'Oh.' Mrs Smiley looked bewildered. With relish the woman explained.

'This place is full of thieves and muggers.'

'Thieves? I thought they were just people shopping.'

'They is – and thieving. They're after one over there, I expect.' The woman nodded knowingly towards two store detectives who were striding with extra long and purposeful strides towards the exit.

Mrs Smiley moved her handbag and gripped the almost empty trolley. She re-entered the food corridors at the Whiskas and Chum section, thinking that she would be less likely to encounter thieves and muggers here. The tins of Bounce, Pal, Pedigree, Please and Mr Dog made her feel more at home. She continued searching, feeling she was in a library filled with food instead of books. But *where* was the tea? Surely they sold tea? Why, she wondered for a second, had Miss Hunter moved to this city where even the salad was washed and cut up for the complicated lives of its eaters.

Around her legs she felt cold breath being breathed out by the freezer cabinets. She glanced up at the second-swallowing clock. It was now a quarter past nine. Despite the chill breath around her legs, she felt hot and flushed: small patches of cloud-shaped pinkness were gathering in her cheeks; she could imagine tall Miss Hunter looming over her. She must have missed the tea *again*. If there weren't so many people she would be able to see better. And if the people were more like shoppers than hunters she would feel more at ease. A trickle of sweat began to creep down her forehead. If only she could ask a shop assistant where things were. She stopped and looked round for one. Something sharp bit painfully into her heels. It was a pushchair, the pusher of which looked as if she had done it on purpose. The pushchair had a transparent cover – a portable green-house on wheels – inside which a baby, instead of a plant, smiled and gurgled soundlessly. It was sealed inside its pram as the food was in its Cellophane. The sight made her feel even hotter. She looked up. There were no windows in the shop – anywhere – just the glass doors. So all the shoppers were sealed in too. She wiped her face. Unbeknown to her, one of the buttons on her artificial belt had come off leaving it dangling. At last she spotted an assistant.

'Can you please tell me where the tea is?'

'Yes, dear. It's on the other side of the disposables.'

'Disposable what?' But the assistant had disappeared. Despite the 'dear', which she found comforting, why was the assistant so sparing with her words? Had they, too, like everything else, been weighed out?

Although she only had Miss Hunter's chicken breast in her trolley, she liked to hold on to its handle; it protected her in a way. Other shoppers' trolleys were piled high with food, and some people had *two* overflowing trolleys. What were they going to do with so much food? Were they fearful lest one minute pang of hunger went unsatisfied? Or was a siege about to take place, and this the last food on earth? All it was, she supposed, was the threat of Easter Monday when the shop would be closed.

She stopped beside a display of Easter eggs. There were Double-Decker eggs and Bounty eggs which contained 'The Taste of Paradise'. Her cousin would never have tasted one of those. Mrs Smiley stretched, and with the tips of her fingers manoeuvred the box towards her; but the box tilted and then fell, the egg knocking her on the head. From nowhere, a supervisor appeared. Mrs Smiley knelt on the ground with the shattered 'Taste of Paradise'.

'I couldn't reach it. I'm ever so sorry,' she apologized to the towering supervisor. Other shoppers gathered round with their great wire trolleys.

'Never mind, madam. These things can happen.'

'But I *will* pay for it.'

'It's all right. It was an accident; I saw that, and we have contingency arrangements for these things.' The supervisor handed Mrs Smiley a replacement egg.

'Thank you ever so much. It's most kind of you.' She held the egg as she would hold a present. 'And I hope you have a happy Eas . . .' She smiled at the empty space which had been filled by the supervisor; then her smile faded, as though an invisible dimmer-switch was attached to the side of her mouth.

Mrs Smiley wheeled her trolley towards a tiled protuberance on which exhausted elderly shoppers perched, their sagging legs drooping towards the floor. She supposed it was a Super Market version of a settee. Small children used its sloping back to practise tobogganing. But there were too many people here, and it was too hot, so she moved towards the freezer cabinets again. From behind, she looked even smaller than when she had entered the shop – though her boots looked bigger, as though she was being swallowed into their big leather troughs.

Feeling momentarily dizzy, she leant against the freezer cabinet, breathing in its invisible frozen breath. Her eyes wandered dazed over its contents until they focused on a large china Easter hare which was filled with paté and reduced to £9.95p. With her forefinger and thumb, she held onto the hare's cold ceramic ears to steady and cool herself. Were the ears filled with paté, too? she wondered vaguely.

She raised her head to look at the clock. It was about to swallow yet another second. She forced herself to move. Whatever happens, she knew she must *not* forget to buy Miss Hunter's seven apples. 'An apple a day keeps the doctor away,' she heard her employer reciting. So into a cul-de-sac where the fruit and vegetables were displayed she went. To her surprise she saw that there were five different types of potatoes.

'Well, I've never seen potatoes like you before,' she chatted to the pre-scrubbed vegetables, feeling a little better. Not wanting anyone to think she was talking to herself, she addressed a pair of hands which had dived in in front of her. 'They're different, aren't they?' The owner of the hands smiled a polite smile instead of talking. Then, inadvertently, Mrs Smiley started a potato avalanche. Over her hands they thundered and bumped, and onto the floor where they rolled away in different directions. She bent to retrieve them, feeling dizzy and stupid. I can't seem to manage in here, she told herself shakily. As she stood up, she caught sight of the first blood-orange she had ever seen. It had been split open to reveal and advertise its dark and bloody interior – so unexpected, so shocking somehow, in spring. She turned away and concentrated on the apples, and a bunch of watercress. Then she forced herself to look at her shopping list. I don't think I can manage any more now. I'll have to come back in the afternoon. I must get out.

She moved towards the check-out counter. A science-fiction implement – a black stethoscope with a claw – was used to feel over the purchases to diagnose their price. It made little bleeping and piping noises which made her feel she had a rash. For a minute she watched the endlessly flowing river of black moving counter taking everything out of the shop which had been brought into it. She placed her items at the edge of the river, observing what the customer in front of her had chosen. Cream Puffs, Hob-nob chocolate biscuits and a Fun Size packet of Aeros, containing twelve per cent extra Free Aero. Had she so little sweetness in her life? Mrs Smiley wondered. The Cream Puff purchaser then took a Next Customer Please divider and placed it firmly between them, fearful, perhaps, lest her puffs might be contaminated by Mrs Smiley's apples. With the barrier safely erected, she looked across it.

Then Mrs Smiley's shopping began its journey. As quickly

as she could, to keep up with the rubber river, she put them into her basket, fumbling and dropping them. It was all too quick for her; towns were too quick for her – for anyone, she thought – and the river had started to consume leaves of Miss Hunter's watercress. Mrs Smiley eyed the glass doors. Soon she would be out, she reassured herself.

'Are these yours? They haven't been weighed yet, have they?'

'Oh, I didn't know you had to do that.'

'The weighing counter is over there, near the vegetables.' Mrs Smiley, feeling as she used to feel at school when she was sent to the back of the class, tried to squeeze past the queue of customers, waiting, barely patiently, behind her.

'It's easier if you go that way. And anyway, you're in the queue for six items or less.' Mrs Smiley looked totally bemused.

'Oh yes, how silly of me.' She hardly dared look at the block-like shoppers.

But where were the scales? She couldn't see anything which resembled scales. In her ears there was a noise, as if the bleeps and squeaks had entered her head.

Aimlessly she wandered once more between the narrowing tunnels of tins. Giant boxes of Bold and Surf reached up to her knees; if she knocked the boxes over, accidentally, she'd be drowned in a tide of unreleased foam.

'Where are the scales? Please,' she whispered to someone who couldn't hear her. Whole sides of Coeur de Brie and Camembert were collapsing, and orange light glistened menacingly inside jars of English marmalade. 'Where are the scales?' she pleaded. The shelves of food were leaning and keeling. She stumbled. Packets of swing-bin liners swung towards her. Regiments of Mr Sheen and Mr Muscle canisters blocked her way. She tottered.

'Are you all right?' She felt a lightweight touch on her

arm and saw a swimming face. Mrs Smiley smiled a ghost
of a smile, pale as skimmed milk. But she couldn't understand what was being said; the words had fallen, empty as
shells around her. And the walls of the shop were beginning
to surge inwards. She was being squeezed between the
waffle-like ceiling and the marble dance floor.

She staggered towards the cake counter where, beside the
inflated meringues and two-tier sponge cakes, she sank
slowly to the ground.

Swiftly two supervisors appeared. Other shoppers stepped
back. Some moved forwards, but then withdrew: one should
not get involved. Into the hot blackness inside Mrs Smiley's
ears came the muffled sound of voices. One of the supervisors was speaking into a telephone built into a pillar.
Within minutes a wheelchair appeared. There were contingency arrangements for such occurrences. One of the female
supervisors flicked the edge of Mrs Smiley's upturned skirt.
Swiftly she was wheeled through the shop, her plastic handbag swinging on the chair handle.

'Imagine,' commented a customer, 'innocently going
shopping, and the next minute you wake up in hospital.'

'*If* you wakes up. I 'ope her name and address is in 'er
'andbag.'

The bandaged glass door was opened and out of the shop
Mrs Smiley was wheeled, to where an ambulance waited,
its one-eyed blue light flashing. On a level with the tethered
dogs she lay. The arms of the boy in the wheelchair (it was
the best place to park him for a morning's shopping) shot
out distractedly, while his revolving-planet eyes scanned the
figure in the wheelchair. The ambulance driver covered
Mrs Smiley's small body with a large, blood-red blanket.

'Thank you. Thank you ever so much,' she mouthed,
before she was slid, like a loaf into a baker's oven, into the
ambulance, and the doors were closed.

Mrs Smiley was driven away.

The Child
Who Couldn't Answer

At six in the morning the house was still submerged in a mist which reached right up to the attic, and came into the window which Miss Jones had left open the night before. It crept everywhere – over her sleeping face, into chairs and up the arms of jumpers.

Later, Miss Jones woke up and heard some children in the street below, walking to school in a line of voices. Miss Jones loved children. She decided to take out for the day an acquaintance's child, who was three or four years old, had blue eyes, a body of silk and belonged to a mother who had four more children.

While Miss Jones dressed, a breeze blew up between the floorboards, and her toes. In winter, and occasionally summer, she hibernated up to her eyes in long scarves, so that for months no one saw her smile. She wore a scarf today.

Miss Jones then had breakfast. She would, she decided, buy a bag of sweets for the small girl who liked her and her sweets. She looked up at the picture which the child had drawn for her. The sun was as large as the flowers on the green-crayon grass, and in a corner, there *she* was, as tall as the grass. She remembered how she had been caressed by the crayon moving over the page. While she remembered, she looked down and saw, reflected in her black coffee, her face – swaying. Quickly she got up.

Miss Jones, tall and strong, walked to the station. The child lived only twenty minutes away, not far from the sea. She would buy the sweets and then collect her. And they would play games which the child would remember, from the first and only other time they had met: Miss Jones's invented games.

Miss Jones sat in the train. Everywhere she went there were children. She looked at the baby opposite, poured into a mould of sleep in its mother's arms. Miss Jones closed her eyes to shut out the sight, and shut out the passing country-side. But the rolling green fields, tilting trees and the child continued to seep into her.

On the other side of her closed eyes, another child started to rattle something, close to her face. Miss Jones lifted a lid and looked at the child, who wore a red hat and danced a doll up and down. She didn't even know the child, and the mother let her continue without saying a word. Carefully she moved the child to the side of her. But the child went on dancing the doll up and down and looking at Miss Jones. If she didn't stop soon, she would push her and her doll under the hot railway-carriage seat. Then the child moved. Miss Jones closed her serious eyes and leant far back in the plush seat, seeking reassurance from it.

Later, she collected the small girl from her home and, holding the whole of her hand in hers, they walked along the street. Miss Jones's red dry hair stuck up and out, ready for kindling under the hot sun.

'Shall we buy celery for tea?' The child agreed. They went into a greengrocer's shop which was filled with the scent of beetroot and with maroon cabbages in full bloom. There was hardly room to breathe or move in the maroon-perfumed vegetable shop. They went out, the child holding onto the arm which hung from Miss Jones's shoulder, and was long and strong, so the child relied on it.

'Can we go to the place where the strawberries are?'

'Perhaps,' Miss Jones answered, for the sake of authority. They walked to the large garden which was owned by an acquaintance of hers, Miss Jones feeling proud of the small girl skipping beside her.

When they arrived, she lifted the strawberry netting and under they went, Miss Jones bent and walking on her knees because the netting was only four feet high. With their knees on the strawberry leaves and their hands full of strawberries, they picked, gathering the English summer into punnets. When the child was filled with fruit and wanted no more, she asked for the game. She was the hen and Miss Jones was the fox, covered in squares of light which came through the netting. They played and chased (Miss Jones sometimes laughing with a cracked laugh as she stumbled after her) until the child asked her to stop: to stop being a fox. But Miss Jones, her red dry hair now almost alight under the sun, just smiled widely, before she caught the child and (only pretending, of course) started to bite her, to eat her up.

'Are you afraid of me?' she asked in a puffed voice. But the child couldn't answer, and ran away from the netting, Miss Jones following her, stooping and dizzy. When she was outside, she caught the child, lifted her up and kissed her face which was covered in strawberry juice. 'You mustn't be frightened of me. We were only playing.' She spoke in low tones, holding the small girl to her. And quietly, and not very surely, she called her 'Darling', and gave her a sweet. The child chewed the sweet, forgot about the fox game and asked for the tree game, which was another of Miss Jones's invented games. Up her tall body the child climbed, using her as a tree to swing on, while hanging from the branches of her hands and peering through the tropical forest of her hair. Then she asked to be put down. She asked again, and was lowered past Miss Jones's serious eyes.

'Can we go home?'

'No – not yet,' Miss Jones answered, smiling high above her head, her smile hidden inside her scarf. Then the child saw a cat sleeping on an onion bed, and ran towards it. While she stroked its purring fur body, Miss Jones smelt the onions whose stems had bent and split, their scent let loose on the air.

They started to walk back to the child's home, her hand held tightly in Miss Jones's. Before they arrived, the child asked if they could go to the playground. Miss Jones consented. So into the deserted playground she ran, and sat on a swing whose long damp ropes disappeared into the branches of a tree. Miss Jones pushed the child, higher and higher into the branches which clanged against each other.

'No more – no more –' the small girl's voice called out. But Miss Jones (perhaps deafened by her scarf) continued to swing her, her arms trembling. Then she told her to jump. The child jumped, causing them both to fall to the ground, unhurt.

'I want to go home,' the child sat up and said.

'Do you?' Miss Jones watched the child's blue eyes open wider. She gave her two sweets. 'Do you love me?' she asked. Before the child started to cry, she gathered her into her arms and rocked her, rocking and rocking until she became still, and kissing her face. The child clung to Miss Jones who was the only other person in the playground. 'We'll go home now, shall we? And have tea – and honey sandwiches.'

She carried the child through the slowly darkening streets, where cool water dripped in the throats of drains.

When they arrived, the child's mother was out. So they had tea, crunching the celery loudly (and smiling) in the silent room. By the hot red light of a gas fire Miss Jones watched the small girl, from deep down in the brown chair in which she sat, her thumbs stuck together with honey.

After a time Miss Jones looked at her watch and asked the child if she would like to go to the sea, before 'Mummy' came home.

'Yes!' said the child, and jumped up and down, singing, 'We're going to the sea! We're going to the sea!' jumping close to Miss Jones's steady face, jumping and jumping until Miss Jones exclaimed 'Stop!' in a voice which filled the room, covering the child. Then quickly she filled the small girl's mouth with three sweets, smiled, and off they set to the seashore.

When they arrived, Miss Jones carried the child into the sea, saying, 'Look! Look!' as she passed through and broke the long lines of waves, the child warm in her arms. Further and further out she waded, until she was up to her waist in the great skirt of the sea. In and out of the water she dipped the child who clung to her, while kissing her salty arms and child-mouth which was filled with sea-water, pressing her to her. Pressing. And the child thought it was still a game. There was no protest, only the child's watching eyes. This amazed and angered Miss Jones. Into the air she lifted the child, who lay suspended and dripping above her, crying, 'I . . .'

From her swaying arms Miss Jones dropped the child into the freezing sea, where she started to sink into the heavy green water.

Miss Jones lifted her feet from the bed of the sea and swam slowly back.

*Out of
the Looking Glass*

Although Mrs Fann, in the following story, and Constance Fann, in the novella, happen to share the same surname (and a few similar qualities), they are not related, and are intended to be quite different characters — though the former was probably the source of the latter.

In the looking glass, in the hall, Mrs Fann appeared, all in purple, whistling in a minor key a major work of Beethoven, while walking down the long passage from the bathroom, her wet hands dripping and slowly drying in the air which made them cold.

She got into bed again, into the sheets and blankets which billowed over her face like waves, and lay still, the green silk counterpane reaching up to her chin, like a lacquered sea.

'I must get up, I must get up, but I can't.' She closed her eyes and slowly, out of the blackness, faces came, close to hers. 'You're insan . . . I can't manage you,' her husband said. 'But it's not your fault,' echoed the smiling faces; faster and faster they came and went. Then her lover without a name appeared, and with two fingers pressed to her lips, she thought she had been kissed,

'Because I am still beautiful.'

It was eleven o'clock. So she stepped out of bed and ate almond-flavoured sweets before combing her hair. With a hairpin, she opened her letters: a letter from her daughter, her lover and a letter from Beethoven; they were all there.

Then she went to the bathroom and had a bath, sitting in the tepid water and washing herself and her clothes, watching the sinking and floating garments, vests and scarves – beautiful things they were – while she smoked a cigarette. She lay in the scented water, almost submerged, like some sea creature; brooding, not thinking. Suddenly she burnt herself and got quickly out of the bath, wetting the whole room.

'Today I shall make a cake.' She started to mix the flour and eggs. 'But I cannot continue, because I hate the smell of flour.' It was choking her, flying up to her face, and her hands were caught in the mixture.

'I must get away!' She ran from the kitchen.

I will go out and buy a whole cream cake which has synthetic cream which imitates badly. I shall eat it before I come home, out in the middle of the green fields where no one will see me eating.

But before I go out I must practise my dancing. Mrs Fann danced by herself, holding on to a dunlopillow cushion (a Christmas present, 'To our dear Mrs Fann, with sincere love'). She danced heavily, her feet in the air, her white socks black when she had finished her polka.

The buttons of my coat must be sewn on. So she safety-pinned them on and went out.

Into the garden she went, with high-stepping feet and luxurious body, the wind round her legs. Quickly she walked past the trees, and the strong light which came through their leaves onto her face. They were shooting light at her; faster and faster it came, making her run, until she reached a public garden.

'I will *not* be shot at by light.' I shall go under the trees where it is green, and my smile will be green, too. I will lie on the hillocks which are slipping and sliding towards me. But if I am not careful where I lie, the great animal hills of delight will roll over me, and I shall be covered in grass and unbroken sod – unable to breathe.

But I must get up, because someone is cutting the lawn; the shears are taking long bites of grass – only a few feet away now – and soon they will catch me up, and my shoe-laces will be cut.

She got up and lit a cigarette. I will smoke my strong cigarettes, so that the smoke flows out on either side of me, like the wake of a ship. I shall not speak to passing dogs, or lift the fallen deck-chairs. I must stand close to the place where men on tall ladders are cutting the damp dead branches of trees, the branches falling and bouncing once on the thin grass. And I shall be beautiful as I walk with my red scarf close to my throat, and my breast high to the wind. But for one moment, before leaving the park, I will sit on this swing, with my gloves on, and then leave the swing, and one glove – the seat swinging, the extended finger pointing from the glove.

Past men I walk, who sit on benches, like stuffed museum birds, staring and speaking sentences to me, perhaps. But I don't hear. I will wave to people, just to puzzle them, and cross the road suddenly, so that the cars will stop, and the dogs that were leaning out of the car windows (gulping and biting pieces out of the air, their eyelashes blown back) will be able to breathe again.

One car stopped and hooted, then another: they were on all sides, hooting and hooting. I am being broken into; the wall which surrounds my silence is being cracked. I must hold on to my walking stick, and put on my hat, so that when I walk under the trees again, their scent will not drown me. Instead I shall smell my own scent (I have forgotten its name), floating beneath my hat. But the cars went on hooting.

'Passion and Death!' she said aloud, and hit the straight lamp-posts with her stick, before putting it into the deepest puddles.

After walking for a little, Mrs Fann went into a fish-monger's shop, where the girl assistant sat terrified and silent behind the till, surrounded by fish, only daring to move when the dead fillets and steaks were returned to the freezer for the night. Mrs Fann smiled at the girl. I will buy nothing; and she walked out of the shop.

I shall not look at Miss Myth who is walking towards me and whom I dislike. She has a little earphone outfit of hair, and knows everything about backward and forward children, and everything else.

Past an advertisement hoarding she went, and then stopped. She was smiling at someone, and someone was watching her. Who? It was the man, in two dimensions, on the poster. He had seen her and he was smiling, too. All day and all night he would smile, until he was torn down: legs, arms and smiling face all crumpled into a litter basket.

I must go home; but I have forgotten the way: I have lived here for thirteen years. I am getting closer to the road I should go up, but I shall not be able to remember its name. So all morning I shall have to hunt for it. I must run, but I can't, because the trees are low and my hair will catch in their branches; so I will have to stoop all the way home. My breathing must be controlled, therefore I shall talk aloud,

'One, two, three.' It is pleasant talking aloud. I might talk all the way home.

Now I know the way. I will lean on the wind, gently now, and pick these tulips, out of the public garden. They must have been planted at night, they were not here before. Perhaps all night long they planted tulips, in flower, cutting them out of boxes, placing them, with green trowels, into the earth, before pressing the squeaking leaves in. Then they would rake between the rows of twenty one way, fourteen the other, never hitting a standing tulip, or leaving footprints in the earth which would be seen and wondered at in the morning. Except, perhaps, for the new gardener, called Young Feasty, who would have left one footprint in the middle of the bed, just for fun, so that he could come back in the morning and smile, while all the other people puzzled – except her. *She* would know – and had now picked a whole bunch of creaking tulips. But who was this head gardener speaking to her, his legs wrapped in sacking and bound with string?

'Madam, the picking of tulips is not permitted. Tres-passers will be prosecuted!' She started to run. I must hurry home and feed my cat. So she left the head gardener, scything with tired arms through the grass, the long swoops and sweeps of the steel cutting the toppling dandelion heads.

In the afternoon, some friends came to tea and, while she lay back in the deck-chair, Mr Fann poured the tea.

'I can't find the cat,' she said. 'Where have you buried the cat?' And all the time she knew that her husband had buried her cat beneath the place where the tea things were laid out: the teapot was close to the spot where her cat lay, still warm.

'But the cat isn't buried; here it is, dear.' Mrs Fann smiled at her guests and lifted the cat onto her lap. It lay there, thinking of birds and quivering, while she held onto its tail and shooed the birds away. She clapped her hands to make them leave the table top and the fence, where they hopped and pecked, tempting the cat with their quick movements and feathered bodies which she was afraid of.

'Go away!' she shouted, but they wouldn't. 'I don't like birds and cats.' She went quickly into her bedroom and lay with her face to the wall . . .

There was a feather on her pillow, close to her face.

'Go away!' But I can't touch it, and blowing it, she knew, would frighten her. Her head was resting on feathers, and at any moment the pillow would burst and there would be feathers everywhere: on her shoulders, caught in her hair, and in her mouth. One day, soon, her husband would say, 'Put your hand into the pillow, dear.' But I cannot and, quickly, before he enters, I must close the bottom of the window; check the slightest breeze which might enter and start the feathers moving, chasing me out of the room: the flutter and chase of cats with feathers in their mouths. She ran out of the room, but ran quickly in again, pursued by her friendly cat.

After some time, she opened the sash window a little, causing thin shavings of air to enter the room. Later she opened it wider, and from her bed looked out at the bottom of the afternoon which came in oblong, from the garden, with lawn, cut short, flowers in profile, the bases of trees, and the long calls of birds which faded when they reached the thin legs of chairs inside her room.

Then a wind came and blew down the posters which were stuck with Sellotape to the wall, splintering the afternoon as they fell to the floor. One by one they fell, with always the interval in between, the time to take breath, the waiting moment for Mrs Fann lying on her bed, before the next picture fell, cracking the silence. When they had all fallen, she got out of bed and slowly Sellotaped them to the walls again, all in different places.

Outside, the guests talked in quiet voices, punctuated by the sound of moving tea things: a cup being placed on a saucer, a teaspoon inside a cup.

'Has she been out today at all?'

'Yes, she went shopping, but forgot to buy anything.'

'Do you still have to do all the housework, so to speak?'

'Well, I do, really, as nothing will rouse her at times, except the alarm clock.'

'Oh dear, I am sorry . . . This is just a suggestion, but wouldn't it really be better for both of you, to cert . . .?' Mr Fann got up quickly and passed the cakes round, again.

Then one of the guests took the alarm clock into Mrs Fann's bedroom, and started to brush her hair, brushing and brushing the tangled hair while watching Mrs Fann's unsmiling face which was turned to the wall.

Suddenly she felt her own long warm hair (which the guest had untied), got up, and asked for some grass to put in her dim bedroom. Mrs Fann arranged the blades of grass in a bowl, but they all fell sideways: not one stood upright. For a long time she tried to make the blades stand upright, while listening to her husband washing up. Faster and faster he put the cups and saucers into the boiling water, then dried them, wearing his wife's apron.

Then the alarm clock went off. Louder and louder in her ears; the whole room became filled with the whirling bells, ringing into her body, hitting her, until she put her hand out into the noise and stopped it.

After some hours, she got out of bed. I will go for a walk under the damp trees; there will be mist all around me and no movement in the leaves. But first I must cover my feet with lavatory paper, taking care that it does not come over the tops of my shoes.

She went out onto the lawn.

Perhaps I will commit suicide – with laughing gas. But what about my clothes, my scarves which are pure purple silk? I shall lie on the stream at the bottom of the garden, and in the morning I will be dead, with Diamond, the gardener, in tears, bending over my body which will still be floating. My stick will be caught in the reeds, moving backwards and sideways, and my hat will be a long way down the stream; and some horse – its tail flowing between its legs – will be looking at it. Then Diamond (who had hit his wife with a bottle four years ago) will lift my beautiful body out of the water. He will tell everybody. It will be a Truth, not a Religious Truth, but shouted from the newspapers. Shouted out in the Albert Hall by my husband, in the middle of a concert, making all the people in rich silks turn their heads slowly. In the back rows, small opera glasses will be raised. Everyone will know.

Instead of committing suicide, I will go home and make love to my husband. But I must tell the voices inside me to 'Stop it, be quiet!', so that I can hear one voice at a time, as I pick flowers at night (when the laurel can become a rose),

my arms stretching over someone else's wall, for del-
phiniums and hollyhocks on the other side.

She started to pick the heavy flowers, gathering and
gathering until she heard the wind move and turn over in
the dark bushes. I can't hold onto the flowers; they are
growing out of my hand.

Mrs Fann dropped the flowers and ran into the house,
along the dark passage until she filled the whole of the
looking glass, before disappearing from sight round a corner.
The looking glass was empty.

Just a small slice of moon was reflected.